To Be
Frank Diego

Dominic Carrillo

CSP Publishing

New York ◆ San Diego

This book is dedicated to my grandparents

ACKNOWLEDGMENTS

Thanks to all friends and family members who've been supportive and helpful throughout the entire writing process, especially Itoro, Bobby, Sarah, John, Rambo, Mario, Alfi, Mike Warren, Matt Reischling, J. Tervalon, Dr. Threatt, Sporkdesigns, the Stefanellis, the Bennetts, Tania, Rollie, and my mom and dad.

What's in a name?
-Shakespeare

To Be Frank

My name is Francisco. It's Francisco Diego Rodriguez in full, but that was cut down to "Frank" a long time ago. The shortening of my name down to one easy syllable happened back in my 4th grade classroom at Immaculate Conception Catholic school.

I remember my teacher looking down at the class roster on the first day back from summer break. She squinted her blue shadowed eyelids in bewilderment as she said my name out loud. Her face appeared to express discomfort at saying my full name all at once, much less pronouncing any part of it correctly. It was okay, I suppose. I couldn't pronounce it much better myself. Though my name was as Mexican as they come, I had never learned how to speak Spanish. I remember my Mexican cousins used to ask me to say my full name to them just so they could laugh when it came out with my nasally vowels and anglicized Rs.

"You must be Spanish, young man," the teacher said.

"No," I replied, "I'm Mexican, I think."

I only added 'I think' because my ethnic identity had never been publicly called into question until that day. I added, 'I think' because I was taught not to talk back or get smart with adults, and this woman was my teacher — an authority. I added 'I think' because I wasn't sure if I fit into one racial category or another.

My teacher's eyes scrunched up again and her brow lowered in what appeared to be disbelief.

"I think you mean you're Spanish," she said, correcting me in front of the entire class.

"I'm pretty sure my dad has never said we're Spanish." I answered as politely as I could, "He says Mexican."

"Well, you don't *look* Mexican," she said, as if it was a complimentary consolation; as if she was saving me from some kind of embarrassment or indignity in front of the rest of my mostly white classmates.

My teacher looked me up and down, maybe guessing that while my father could have been Mexican, my mother was probably white. My mom *is* white—a mix of German, Irish and English, which simply amounts to 'white' in the United States of America.

I was in the unique and confusing position of having to choose one ethnic identity that day in 4th grade. I chose Mexican, and I made that declaration to myself, my teacher, and to the entire class. But apparently my small stand didn't matter. Unbeknownst to me, I was about to be officially mainstreamed into Frank; de-cultured Frank; simple and safe Frank.

"Okay then Fran-see-sco," she struggled, " —may I just call you Frank?"

"Yeah," I said. I was a kid. I wasn't about to be directly defiant and say 'No' to my teacher—especially not on the first day of school. I also said 'Yeah' because I had no idea I would turn into *Frank* for the rest of my life.

That teacher's name was Ms. Fernandez — Megan Fernandez if I remember correctly. She had bleached blonde hair with darker brown roots, and she couldn't

even pronounce her own last name with the right accent —
kind of like me. I guessed she was half-Mexican too, but
might have been ashamed to admit it.

Like many others, including myself, Ms. Fernandez took
the easy road and called me 'Frank' for the rest of the
school year. It stuck with my teachers and friends, then
gradually sunk in with my family too.

But that little scene happened over twenty years ago.

For whatever reason, it was the first thing I thought
about as I entered the kitchen in my parents' house. It was
around 10am. I was 33 years old. It was the beginning of
the day that my life dramatically changed, and the last
time anyone has called me Frank.

Morning in Diego

There was a perfectly good reason why I started that particular weekday morning sitting at the dining room table at my parents' house. Like other grown children, I still counted on my parents for certain things: a decent present at Christmas, a semi-embarrassing voicemail on my birthday, and a ride across town when my car was in the shop. And they were usually predictable on these such occasions.

That day my Volkswagen was at a mechanic's shop in Pacific Beach, on the other side of the city. I hadn't talked to my parents or inquired about needing a ride that morning, but that was usually unnecessary. They were my parents. They were retired. They practically never left the house unless they were walking around the neighborhood, going to buy weekly grocery specials, or traveling with other fanny-pack-carrying tour groups.

And it was nice, at first, to sit there at the family table all by myself with my cereal, coffee, and a fresh newspaper. The table reminded me of my childhood, yet there was no older brother or sister there to ridicule me, or pose sardonic questions in an effort to ruin my appetite. No dad to break the awkward silences by mentioning the painfully obvious. No mom to offer, and excessively re-offer, heaping plates of food. I was picturing the old days, before my two siblings moved out and had families of their own. Now it was only my parents who were unexpectedly absent from their own home.

My question concerning their whereabouts was answered when my mom called me about ten minutes later. She was still my only parent with a cell phone. It seemed my dad had been actively avoiding technological advances — aside from keeping up with the basic functions of a TV remote control — since the late 1970's.

"Good morning, Frank," she said.

"Hey, where are you guys?" I asked.

"I was just calling to make sure you knew we were out of town for a few days in case you needed anything."

"Well, I kind of did need a ride," I said. "But it's too late for that I guess."

"Oh, I'm sorry," my mom said. "Is there enough food in the fridge?" She seemed to assume that the solution to life's problems centered around eating.

"Yes, but... It wasn't food-related." I said.

"Well there's that roast chicken and the leftover pasta thing I made two days ago."

"OK," I said, realizing she was going to say what she wanted to say regardless.

"It should still be fresh, and I made some sweet iced tea too..." she added.

"OK, thanks."

"Is everything OK?" she asked.

"Yes, mom. It's just that I was —

"Slow down! Jesus Christ!" she yelled, presumably at my dad who must have been driving. She continued talking without remembering she'd cut me off.

Continuing with a string of questions, she completely ignored my attempt to explain my situation. In a kind, motherly way, she went on to demand repeated assurances of my well-being, which were then followed by domestic inquiries of no circumstance whatsoever. Somewhere in between her recitation of the refrigerator's inventory and backseat-driver side comments, she told me that they were on their way to Santa Barbara for the next few days.

"All right, goodbye, Frank."

"See you later."

"OK. Bye," she repeated.

That's how our brief conversation ended, as usual, with my mom saying "goodbye" in about five different ways before finally ending the call.

So my main purpose for being at my parents house was already screwed. I had taken the entire *day off* to pick up my car and run a few errands. But now, I was at my parents' house with no way to pick up my car. I was alone and stranded without a vehicle—a major obstacle to movement (a disability; a social embarrassment, really) in Southern California.

Another possibility, Kate—who I was still referring to as *my girlfriend* – had already gone to work. She was an elementary school teacher, and I wasn't about to interrupt her lessons to trouble her for a ride. I sensed that my emails and texts were annoying her of late anyway. Either way, I didn't have the audacity to inconvenience her, or anyone, merely to give me a ride to PB.

So would I opt for public transportation? Had I ever taken a San Diego bus before?

I put my dilemma off for a minute and turned my attention back to the newspaper lying in front of me. As usual, I had to search for substance in the back section's articles: *Oil Spill Off the Coast, Israelis Strike Back, Bombing in Baghdad, GM Record Lay-Offs.* These stories had once graced the front-page, but had since taken a backseat to more pressing local news. The San Diego headline of the day was this:

'TORREY PINES TREE TOPPLES'

Jesus Christ, was a tree really worthy of the front page? Did the fallen pine kill somebody or what? Weren't thousands dying in foreign wars — the economy on the verge of collapse?

But it turned out that felled pine tree was a really important one — on a famous championship golf course. According to the writer, the tree was historic, a 'defining,' 'marquee' landmark. It was a 'devastating loss'. That and other sports-related stories — such as *The Chargers Bolt Back* — seemed to alleviate and distract those who would rather not focus on more significant, global events. Maybe San Diego had a knack for promoting and fostering a sense of insulated contentment.

And the oil keeps spilling. But it's playoff season, so the entire back page, in huge black letters, said this:

GO CHARGERS!

The Shapes of Women

Without yet feeling any sense of urgency, I did what I've always done after eating breakfast and drinking coffee: I went straight to the bathroom. Normally, I'd leave out the banal details of my post-café toilet time (and, I assure you, I have no intention of sharing any unpleasant specifics here). However, my bathroom visit that morning reminded me of the 'Playboy factor' — the relevance of which I had neglected for years.

It's no secret within my immediate family that catalogs of Playboy magazines have been poorly hidden in the recesses of our bathroom cabinet for decades. So when I sat down on the toilet that morning, and habit led my eyes in the direction of the cabinet, I was reminded of how I had first discovered what naked women looked like.

It happened when I was in first grade. My friend John and I were creating a childhood fortress on the canyon slope just beyond my backyard. We needed tools to clear brush and reinforce our stronghold against our imagined enemy, so we spent one afternoon searching through the dark, dusty cabinets in the garage. While scavenging, I came across an unmarked box of magazines. The cover was face up. It featured a busty brunette wearing a skimpy, American flag patterned bikini. I had never seen any book or magazine like it. The colors on the cover were faded and the pages stiff with age. Across the top it said: PLAYBOY. I had no idea what the word Playboy meant.

"Check this out," I whispered to John.

His eyes widened. "Put that away," he said. "You're gonna' get us busted."

I ignored his warning. I put the Playboy under my shirt and sprinted back to the fort. John followed me. His curiosity seemed to trump his disapproval. As he looked over my shoulder, I discovered the pictures and lewd cartoons, and we giggled as only first graders would at the sight of nude and seminude women. Our commentary and focus centered on the various shapes and sizes of boobies. That's what we called them: *Boobies*. And they were fascinating. Though John was initially skeptical and questioned both the wisdom and morality of taking my dad's old Playboy magazines, we immediately launched our new mission.

'Operation Playboy' — a secret mission to smuggle Playboys from the garage to our outdoor fort without detection. The mission offered both risk and reward. After we scanned through adult cartoons, examined pictures of half-naked ladies, giddily commented on their boobies, and generally admired their beautiful shapes, we would return them to their boxes in the garage cabinet. Occasionally we'd keep one, wrap it in plastic, and bury it for future viewing.

Operation Playboy continued for more than a decade. The only change was that the hiding place for the magazines shifted from the fort to my bedroom; from plastic protected burial to strategic placement under my bed. Later, during my adolescence, I came upon another goldmine stacked in back of the bathroom cabinet — a stash that I continued to reference for years.

At the time, the thing I appreciated about Playboy (and I assumed this is why my dad's been a subscriber since 1972) is that they were never really pornographic. They were only semi-pornographic. And the women in the featured pictorials were unrealistically beautiful, their bodies flawless.

Only later did I realize that Playboy objectified female bodies; and that the playmates were almost always of European descent (never Mexican, or even half-Mexican — aside from the rare "Hot and Spicy" Latin ladies issue).

Unfortunately, my habit of perusing Playboy likely warped my perception of reality when it came to the types and shapes of real women in real life. Sometimes it made me wonder how it affected the way I viewed Kate, and women, and beauty in general. So maybe Operation Playboy turned out to be a bad idea after all.

That morning, in my parents' bathroom, I realized I had mostly outgrown my penchant for Playboy viewing. But I also admitted that I hadn't outgrown my appreciation for the shapes of women, along with my somewhat warped perception of them.

Sans Technology

Though I'd never ridden a city bus before, the only reasonable solution to my car problem would be to use public transportation or my own two feet—both of which I considered inconvenient, if not socially demeaning. But there was no logical alternative. A taxi would be way too expensive. I only needed to get to Pacific Beach by seven, before the mechanic's shop closed, which sounded simple enough. So I rubbed some sunscreen on my nose, threw a sweatshirt in a small backpack, and locked the back door on my way out.

I started with a shortcut-- walking down the canyon path toward the trolley stop on SDSU's campus. I had taken the trolley once before and I knew the SDSU stop was less than a mile away, with a line that headed west toward the beach. I figured I could start with the trolley, then figure out which bus would get me to Pacific Beach.

As I hit the canyon trail and smelled the aroma of eucalyptus leaves, I felt kind of embarrassed that I'd never once used the city bus system. Figuring out the routes and the bus numbers might be challenging, I thought, but how difficult could it be?

At that point, if Kate was with me, she would've laughed at my primitive navigational plan. Compared to me, she was a different kind of rational and technological being. For instance, before I finished describing my geographic dilemma, she would have googled the best route, multiple transit sources and all accompanying instructional details on her phone or laptop.

When it came to ignorance about technology, Kate referred to me as Cro-Magnon Man. True, I had failed to keep up. For example, I was notorious for neglecting to recharge my cheap, featureless cell phone on a regular basis— occasionally alienating those who counted on immediate responses to calls, texts, and emails. Though she found this "cute" at first, it came to visibly annoy her over the years.

I looked at my cell phone and noticed it was about to die. So it looked to be another 'old school' day for me, which was fine. Sometimes I preferred the simplicity. Sometimes I didn't want to know which calls I missed, send text notes back and forth like a teenager bored in class, or be expected to promptly respond to everyone every single minute of the day.

— Hadn't I said that same exact thing to Kate once?

A day outside, *sans* technology, seemed refreshing. After all, I knew San Diego's landscape very well. No GPS necessary, I thought, I was born and raised here. And aside from two years of graduate school in LA, I had never lived anywhere else in my entire life—nor had I ever planned to.

The Midpoint

Minutes into the canyon walk, when I had reached the midpoint of the dirt path, I paused. The trail looked much smaller than I remembered it. Most of the big trees were gone. And I was standing in a spot where I'd never felt comfortable venturing beyond as a child. I wondered why I had been scared to go past it, because there was nothing really frightening there — other than the fact that it was another hundred yards further away from home.

Continuing on, I inadvertently kicked up dirt with my slightly pigeon-toed left foot as I made it toward the end of the canyon. The trail had narrowed and tall, sticky fern-like plants brushed against my arms. A squadron of tiny bugs buzzed by my ears and flew in my face. I clumsily swatted at them and tried to avoid the branches as I crept through. The smell of fresh foliage was so thick it made me sneeze and cover my nose.

As I picked up my pace, I was reminded of how distanced I was from my Indian roots. Although I had no evidence of direct lineage to the Kumeyaay Indians of San Diego, I'd seen old black and white pictures of these indigenous people. They looked much like Indians from northern Mexico. My grandfather was a Yaqui Indian from northern Mexico, so I felt connected somehow. But inching through those wild bushes and hundreds of bugs was too much.

I wanted a Jamba Juice. I wanted to be insect free. I hungered for a paved sidewalk. And I imagined that my

Yaqui ancestors would have kicked my ass if they knew me.

A patch of bamboo trees marked the area where the winding dirt trail wedged between the fences of two single-story homes and ended on the sidewalk of Campus Avenue. Strange as it may sound, that bamboo reminded me of the Vietnam War—or the Vietnam that I had imagined and re-lived in the canyon years ago. It was where I fought my childhood wars with fake guns that looked way too real to be toys. Back then I'd created a highly fictionalized version of war that was based on a real war fought in a real country that killed millions. I'd watched too many Rambo movies as a kid.

I glanced back at that speck of wilderness in the midst of dated suburban sprawl and considered that I had learned and unlearned much since I was a child. But at times I still felt like that little brown-haired, pigeon-toed kid with a bowl cut, quoting lines from Rambo, getting lost in the combat zone, yet feeling too scared to explore the whole thing—to go past the midpoint. I suppose that morning the canyon reminded me that I was much older than I used to be, but not necessarily much wiser.

Maybe it was because I had passed the canyon's midpoint, for once, without any fear. Maybe it was that I'd embarked on something outside of my routine that day. But I was beginning to recognize that my biggest enemy was no longer an imaginary Viet Cong soldier, or an irritating insect.

It was me.

Which, in retrospect, may have been the reason why I ended up handcuffed in the back of a police car later that day.

Kate

On the uphill trek to SDSU, I checked my phone. The battery symbol was blinking and I realized the charger was still inside my car in PB. So I sent Kate a quick text message. I wanted to confirm our meeting that night because she hadn't responded to my last message — or the email before that.

The text read: "Gringos @7pm PB?"

I pushed send.

There is, in fact, a Mexican restaurant called Gringos, and there's really no irony there. It caters specifically to the gringos who are willing to pay a lot of money for "elevated" Mexican food, made and served in Pacific Beach in the Latino image that stylish, trendy, California gringos appreciate most. That is, an imagined one.

But would Kate even read or respond to my text?

I pictured Kate teaching in her classroom at that moment. She would have probably been irritated by the ring or even the buzz of a vibrating phone interrupting her class. But I had no choice. She was so dedicated to teaching, she might just ignore any communication from the outside world until after work. To her, teaching was sacred and those little 5th graders didn't realize how lucky they were to have Miss Kate as their teacher. She was not only caring, but also extremely intelligent and thought provoking — I'm sure. I guessed so. I had never been in her classroom. I had never really asked her too much about it either, but I could tell by the way she talked about her students. In fact, if I was actually paying attention to her stories about her lessons, she'd make me feel like I was bad at my job.

And I probably was. I told her that once, but she reassured me that I was being hypercritical of myself again; that I was highlighting the negatives and downplaying the positives. Then I would suggest to her that I was being humble. Then she'd say something about my false modesty. She was probably right about that too.

I was also critical of Kate, though I kept it to myself. My silent criticisms were usually way too amorphous to say out loud anyway. In the imaginary discussions I'd have with her, the words 'tone' and 'vibe' and 'demeanor' would repeatedly come up in my attempts to describe her problem. But then, if I'd implied that she had a problem out loud, she would have asked me something like: 'So this is a problem *I* have?' And she would have said it with this entitled tone, as if she were so refined and educated and special that she could never actually have a problem. At that point I'd realize that I shouldn't have used the word 'problem' because her general way of being was not necessarily a thing to be fixed, or that could be fixed. And I had my own problems. Who was I to speak? So I didn't. Not on that particular topic at least.

I could no longer suppress my thoughts about Kate. *Why was I still calling her my girlfriend? Hadn't the end been crystal clear?* I had become quietly consumed with memories of her, which partially explained why I wasn't paying much attention to my physical surroundings as I walked toward SDSU: the flat sidewalk path flanked by mostly student-rented houses with unkept yards; an occasional empty beer can faded from the sun; a skinny palm tree piercing the clear blue skyline. There were no students in sight because it was the middle of January, and SDSU was still on winter break.

And the weather — generally sunny, mild and comfortable year-round — was noticed by visitors, but not by most San Diegans. It would go largely unappreciated until that rare rainy day, or that string of cloudy days that weren't "ideal." Then many would complain, and the Barbie and Ken weather reporters would read their cue cards to apologize for the imperfect weather — as if we'd all been promised clear and sunny forecasts everyday in America's self-proclaimed "finest city."

Well, it wasn't one of those atypical weather days. It was about 75 degrees with a pleasant breeze and a brightly shining sun. The weather *was* nearly perfect in San Diego. The weather wasn't the problem here.

I reached in my pocket and clicked open my phone to see if Kate had replied in the last few minutes. Orange and white graphics streamed down the screen before it went black. My cell phone was officially dead. I pictured Kate trying to respond and being directed to an automated message, or nothing at all. I hoped my lack of cell phone communication wouldn't bother her as much as it usually did.

Maybe that was part of my problem, I thought. That I never communicated enough; that I censored myself too much with Kate. At the very least, I was trying to figure out what it was that had made me feel so disconnected from her, unable to picture us happily married — after three years of content and comfortable dating.

Go Aztecs!

As I made it to the bottom of the escalator at the nearly empty SDSU trolley stop, I noticed a large black and red banner with the new school mascot on it that said:

Go Aztecs!

It reminded me of the first and only time I was ever on television. My fifteen seconds of fame. It happened during the big controversy over the SDSU mascot back when I was in college. It had to do with the human version of the Aztec mascot 'looking Mexican' or not. Of course, the state university was very concerned with accuracy. After all, the school mascot took its name from Mexican warriors who had fought against Spanish invaders almost two thousand miles south of San Diego, in a vastly different geographic and cultural setting—but that was beside the point.

"Go *Kumeyaay*!" didn't sound as cool.

So, the image of the mascot had evolved over the years—from a baton-twirling white cheerleader in Sioux Indian headdress to a darker-skinned, Roman-nosed, male Aztec profile. The problem was that the human incarnation of the mascot, who ran around at sporting events and blew out of a conch shell and yelled *Go Aztecs!*, had not similarly evolved. He was a muscular, spray-tanned white guy in a cheap imitation Aztec costume.

That's when some concerned students, mostly those of Mexican descent, decided to challenge the white Aztec. The university was receptive to them, most certainly

18

because they were so concerned with historical accuracy —
and public relations. A lot of people who called
themselves a variety of things for a variety of reasons —
Mexican, Latino(a), Chicano(a), Hispanics and Others —
protested publicly, speaking on the news about the
injustice of it all. That's when I had my fifteen seconds of
TV fame.

I was walking by the Channel 8 news crew on campus
when a reporter with a wireless microphone, big fake
smile, and a distracting amount of foundation on his face
approached me.

"Excuse me young man, can I get a quote from you
about the mascot controversy?" he asked.

"Sure." I said. I was caught off guard and somewhat
detached from the mainstream debate, but not about to
pass up an opportunity to be on local television.

"Ok. Let's roll here," he said to the cameraman, then
used his index finger to comb back his eyebrows. He took
a deep breath and put on his best anchor voice:

"Good evening, San Diego. Live here on SDSU's
campus, talking to students about the enormous
controversy ignited over the university's mascot." Then he
turned to me and asked:

"What do you think about the race or ethnicity of the
Aztec mascot?"

"Well, which one," I asked back, "Race or ethnicity?"

"Oh, race, I suppose," he answered, noticeably irked.

"To be honest, I try to avoid racial categorization if
possible," I said.

"May I ask you what your racial background is? Are you Mexican, white…?"

"Uh, I'm both." I said.

"Huh. So I suppose that puts you somewhere in the middle, eh?" the reporter asked.

"Well, yeah, I guess it's confused me off and on throughout my life," I said, "but I don't think it has any real bearing on my view about the school's mascot. It has a lot more to do with history — "

I must have used the word 'bearing' to try to sound sophisticated on TV. I remember thinking that the issue wasn't so simple, yet I was ready to explain my whole perspective on the matter. Too bad I was sharply cut off at 'history.'

That's when the reporter lowered the microphone, sighed, disingenuously smiled at me, shook his head a little, and walked toward his crew. I guess I didn't interview well, I thought. I remember seeing myself that night on the news. My fifteen seconds looked and felt more infamous than famous. They'd edited my part down to only my first response — a stunted blurb that made me sound like an apolitical, apathetic frat boy. I felt I'd been misrepresented.

But several weeks after the news articles and campus protests and such, the university committee decided to ensure that the next human version of the Aztec mascot, when competing with others of equal yelling and conch-blowing ability, should be darker-skinned, and preferably of Central American indigenous descent.

Go Aztecs!

That banner dominated the huge wall of the nearly-vacant trolley terminal, almost obscuring a smaller, official looking sign that read: "This Area For Ticket Holding Passengers Only."

Jesus Christ, I hadn't bought a ticket yet!

At that moment, I heard light rail noise coming from the tunnel on my left. Standing on the yellow line that I wasn't supposed to cross over, I peered down the tunnel and saw the lights from the trolley. I turned around and scanned the area for a ticket-dispensing machine. Nothing. The ticket machine must have been on the street level — up the escalators, around the corner, and up another flight of stairs. If I went upstairs to buy ticket, I'd be waiting another 45 minutes for the next train. And I didn't want to sit there and waste time.

The bright red trolley glided into the terminal. As it slowed down I looked through its windows. The entire train was occupied by less than a dozen people, and I didn't see anyone inside who looked like a uniformed conductor.

The doors slid open and made a futuristic beeping sound. *The future is now.* Nobody else was around to ask about tickets. *Would anyone even check to see if I had one? Couldn't I just buy a ticket on board if it became an issue?* Public transit wasn't exactly my field of expertise. Then the trolley door made another soft beeping noise, warning me that I had no time for internal debate.

I bolted toward the sliding doors, slipped in, and grabbed a silver handrail. I realized I was holding it too tightly as the trolley left the station. The movement was not as abrupt as I'd expected. It was surprisingly smooth — as I had assumed the rest of my trip to PB would be.

Carl

As I relaxed my grip on the handrail, I looked at the trolley route posted above the window. It was pretty simple. There were only three lines in all of San Diego County. I was on the westbound one. But I felt more like I was on the monorail at Disneyland than a real city metro. The trolley car was empty except for an older black man sitting two rows away from me. We exchanged glances as he caught me staring at the logo on his designer cashmere sweater.

"How you doin?" he said.

"Pretty good, thanks."

"Know where you goin'?" he asked. I wondered if I looked as green to public transportation as I felt.

"Ehh, not really, to be completely honest," I said.

He laughed out loud, a deep and rich sound that resonated down the empty aisles. I found humor in being unsure sometimes, but didn't intend for it to be that funny. I considered whether or not I should be offended.

"Ha-ha. Well, nobody really knows, do they," he said, "Unless, of course, they walk with the Lord."

Oh, Jesus. Was this guy a Bible-thumper? Would the reminder of Catholic school never end? — That's how I would usually react to such references to 'the Lord.' However — maybe it was the laugh or because I was reminded of

Morgan Freeman—I figured this guy put more faith in this life and its experiences than the afterlife and judgment day and ghosts and goblins. His forehead lines were deep with age, but the rest of his face looked relatively young. It was only his gray hair that put him over the age of fifty.

"How old are you, kid?" he asked.

"Thirty-three," I said. It must have been the first time I had said my age out loud in a while. It didn't make me feel like a kid. It made me feel old.

"Ah," he furrowed his brow a bit, "older than I thought."

"How about you?" I asked, thinking it might make me feel young again. He had started this anyways.

"Just turned sixty-five," he said with pride.

"Amazing." I said. It really was. When my grandfather was in his sixties, he looked like he had one foot in the grave. But this guy looked ready to arm wrestle me or challenge me to a basketball game—and win.

"What's your name?" he asked.

"Frank," I said, "Yours?"

"Carl," he smiled, extending his thick, wrinkled hand. I didn't usually shake hands with strangers aboard public transit, but then again, I didn't normally use public transportation. I extended my smaller, more slender arm and hand.

"Good to meet you," I said.

Bright sunlight greeted us as the trolley made its way out of the tunnel and into Mission Valley. We eased into the first stop: Grantsville. Only two people entered the trolley there—an elevated concrete strip above a huge parking lot alongside the noisy traffic of the interstate freeway. It seemed to be a uniquely modern no-man's land. The soft beeping repeated and the doors closed. We continued westward.

"Nice weather today," he said. I guessed he wasn't from San Diego.

"Yeah. Pretty sunny," I said. It was mundane commentary, but the weather had already crossed my mind and Carl had put me in a talkative mood.

"Ain't nothin' compared to Birmingham in the summer," Carl said.

"Are you from there?" I asked.

"Yes, sir. Marched there with Dr. King in 63'," he said.

As Carl continued to speak, I wondered if what he was telling me was an oft-told tale, full of elaborations, and perhaps, imagined memories that time had turned into fabrications. But I didn't mind. Maybe it was the convincing tone of his voice, or his way of presenting only the highlights. Maybe it was that I had no one else to talk to.

To my surprise, at first he gave no more than a slight mention to the indignities of segregation in the South, Bull Connor and his attack dogs and fire hoses—even his meeting Dr. Martin Luther King in a church to hear a speech on non-violent protest. He sped through all that, then leaned forward and said, "You know what the best thing was though?"

I looked at him and opened my eyes a bit wider, indicating that I was clueless.

"The girls," he told me. "See, I was about 16 years old and I'd never been around so many girls my age — pretty girls. We were all shoved in those jail cells — packed in — and I was smashed in between two beautiful young ladies all night. Mmmm."

For a moment, he seemed to become lost in the memory of that hormone-filled jail cell. A big smile spread on his face, then his eyes moved back to me with a more serious reality check.

"Don't get me wrong though," he added. "Bull Connor and them scared the mess outta' me. Why, they beat the *cuss* outta' my friend Earl. Oooh, I remember that."

Carl cringed. So did I.

"But I'll never forget those girls. Mmmm," he repeated.

The trolley slowed down for the next stop. It was the Mission stop. The doors opened but nobody exited or entered. The trolley speakers made a short rattling noise that sounded like the ring of an alarm. We didn't budge.

"So you wanted to get out of Alabama, huh?" I asked.

"Yes, indeed. Got the cuss outta' there. Got a *scholah-ship* to play football here, running back at SDSU… Ohhh, back in early… back in '65. We weren't too bad then, and it paid for my education — got me outta' Alabama at least."

"What do you think about the Aztec mascot?" I couldn't resist.

"The Mexican one or the white one?" he said.

"I don't know — either one."

"Ha—if they goin' for accurate representation, if they wanna' give credit where credit is due, they should make that fake costume-wearing Aztec black!" Carl laughed at himself. "Look at the basketball and football programs—the biggest ones—where all the money is. They all black players—almost all black." He chuckled.

So did I, maybe just a bit awkwardly.

The trolley wasn't moving. *What was going on?* The doors remained wide open, but not a single person was waiting to get on.

"Them Mexicans don't have cuss to complain about though, compared to what I been through," he said. Then he self-edited, "I'm sorry, you're not Mexican are you?

"Yes, I am actually." I said. "Half."

"I thought I saw a little somethin' Latin in you, " Carl said. "Somethin' around the eyes."

I nodded in agreement. I usually liked it when someone thought I was Mexican, or half Mexican, or anything besides being only white. I was both Mexican and white—never fully one or the other. And whenever someone wanted to place me in the "white only" category—to make things easier—it made me recoil and cling to what little indigenous roots I had. *Even if the Yaqui would've kicked my ass if—*

The trolley remained motionless. Something wasn't right. Carl perked his head up and turned like a watchdog. He appeared to be searching for someone outside, someone coming from the front of the trolley. I couldn't see anyone approaching from my angle.

"Waiting for someone?" I asked.

"Just the meter maid," he said as he reached into his pocket. "You know: the trolley *po-lice*."

I turned my head around and still couldn't spot anyone. I hoped Carl was wrong as I reached into my pocket, as if I might miraculously find a ticket in there.

"Do you see them coming, or just guessing?" I asked.

"Well, I ride this trolley almost everyday. And if you've lived my life, son, you learn to pay attention to little things — to be very aware in order to get by," he said, with a greater sense of gravity.

"Like in Alabama in 1963?" I followed up.

"And Vietnam in 1969," he replied, and raised both eyebrows in acknowledgement of our approaching visitor.

Vietnam? It sounded like a stretch — an opportunity for Carl to reveal another interesting biographical tidbit. But I didn't have any time to contemplate the breadth of Carl's experiences. I turned my head and saw the trolley police officer entering authoritatively through our section's doors. He went to Carl first and asked for his ticket. Carl, ready with it in hand, showed him. Then the officer turned to me.

"Your ticket?" he asked.

"Uh, well," I said, almost stuttering, "I didn't have a chance to buy one because I didn't know the machine…" The words coming out of my mouth became fragmented and incoherent: "No ticket… doors closing…my first time… Chargers game… I have money to buy a ticket."

The mustached officer shook his head at my pathetic attempt to explain my situation. I thought he might have mercy on me, but I had no such luck. Even Carl lacked sympathy.

"Couldn't buy a ticket, son?" Carl said, shaking his head, with a mix of surprise and disappointment.

The officer showed even less understanding.

"I'm not taking your money, buddy," he said condescendingly. "Get off, go to the machine, and *figure it out*!"

I got off and was left standing at a desolate terminal stop as the trolley sailed west without me. I didn't have a chance to say goodbye to Carl—not even a silent, acknowledging nod.

I turned around and stared at a red and white machine. It said "San Diego MTS" on the top in bold letters. I didn't know what MTS stood for, but gathered that it was the machine that dispensed trolley tickets. '*Figure it out!*' echoed back at me. The sun beat down on my face.

I slid my credit card in the machine and studied the unfamiliar options, but cancelled the transaction once I realized I didn't know what the hell I was doing. *Cro-Magnon man.* And there wasn't a single person around to ask.

Church bells rang faintly in the distance. I peeked over the machine and noticed that the comforting, old world sounds were coming from the Mission Basilica less than a mile away. This put the time at eleven o'clock.

In all my years living in San Diego, celebrated and promoted for its highly fictionalized Spanish colonial past, I had never been to the mission. It was by far the oldest rebuilt historical building in town, and history was my thing. I looked at the schedule on the display board and realized the times and destinations were beginning to make sense. If I was reading it right, I had forty minutes before the next trolley would arrive.

I knew I didn't want to wait around that long. Already, I had cupped one hand above my nose to shield it from the sun. I was paranoid about skin cancer. Forty minutes, I thought. So I moved in the direction of the sonorous bells — toward history.

The Mission

It was a short walk. A long flight of stairs led up to the mission entrance from the street level, dissecting a slope covered in dark green ice plant. Pink flowers poked out here and there, and bees buzzed at their tops.

As I climbed the stairs, I couldn't help but picture colonized Kumeyaay Indians manicuring and watering all the imported flowers and plants. I imagined the Spanish priests, or Padres, justifying forced Indian labor as necessary penance to the Lord: a reasonable punishment for years of pagan idolatry — the guilt that paid dividends, and gave the priests more free time to pray and get weird. At the top of the stairs I noticed a gardener mowing the lawn. He was a dark-skinned, short Mexican man. I wondered if he were a Kumeyaay descendant, and if he felt grateful or penitent to the church — or just underpaid and exploited.

From the front, the mission looked small — freshly painted white, its grounds well kept. I strolled along the thick-walled portico. Every ten feet, small wood carvings of Catholic saints were placed in alcoves behind bronze bars. I paused and spent a few moments studying the face of San Francisco, also known as Saint Francis of Assisi. The sharp cuts and harsh lines in the carving made it look as if he had a strong sense of purpose, but had struggled to reach it; perhaps he even lost sight of it at one point — suffering quietly along the way; having devoted his life to a vision that others could not (or refused to) see. At least that's what I wondered about him.

I also wondered if anyone ever called him "Frank."

When I reached the end of the terracotta tiled corridor, I noticed it wasn't a path to the mission's entrance. Instead it dead-ended at a flagpole with a large plaque at the base of it. The plaque was dedicated to a mission priest — a padre — who had died very close to that same spot. But he hadn't died defending a Kumeyaay Indian. Nor had he died of over-exhaustion from gardening all day.

The padre had died in 1775 at the hands of Kumeyaay Indians who were revolting against the mistreatment and forced labor imposed on them by the priests. They also revolted because the priests were unable to keep their promise to the Indians that they wouldn't be raped and pillaged by Spanish soldiers. The Kumeyaay revolted because they were tired of the treachery and oppression of colonization. They revolted because who-knows-what else the Spanish did to them.

Of course, it didn't say all that on the plaque. I remembered the extended version of the story from a history book I'd read after I graduated from college.

I walked back under the portico and found the entrance to the mission. A few tourists walked out. That's when I noticed there was an admission fee. I wasn't sure I wanted to pay to get in, nor did I have time to be a tourist. From where I stood I could see everything inside: the church, the cemetery, the Indian dormitories. Not one building was original. They had been rebuilt, restored and kept immaculate by the almighty Catholic Church. Apparently, the Church still had enough power and money — despite all the million dollar lawsuits they'd lost because a few of the padres had problems keeping their hands off of little children (and some adults).

There was once a priest like that at Immaculate Conception Catholic school. He never touched me or my friends, but he was later accused of molesting a few students and "inappropriately touching" a woman who came to confess to him one evening. That woman clearly didn't like being handled by a priest, and was brave enough to report him. But the priest didn't fess up once the news became public. Instead, he repeatedly denied her accusations and the allegations of others who stepped forward.

A long time ago, during a religion class, this same priest told me that if my parents and I didn't go to Catholic mass every Sunday, then we would all eventually go to hell, regardless if we were good people or not. Then he quoted the Bible to support his claim.

So, standing there at the entrance, I decided I wasn't about to give three dollars to the Church's molestation trial fund just to see a reconstructed, unimpressive mission. Instead I turned and entered the gift shop to see if I could find any pictures of historical items I might have found inside the mission I'd just decided to boycott.

The shop was nearly empty, except for a preppy, Gap-attired couple casually browsing through postcards. When they passed me on their way out, I heard the wife say, "Do you want to grab a coffee now, hon?" But the tone of her voice implied that it wasn't so much a question as it was a demand. *She* wanted coffee, and only wished her husband to co-sign on the deal for good measure.

She reminded me of Kate. I could remember times when I noticed her subtle tactics of control emerge in the form of innocent questions or indirect suggestions. It only bothered me sometimes — when I was paying attention closely enough to notice.

And it was the mention of coffee that reminded me of the first time Kate and I went on a date. Well, it wasn't really supposed to be a date. A mutual friend of ours had quietly intended for us to meet at a happy hour, and we ended up getting along well and talking all night. It was the first time in a while that I was truly engaged in a conversation with a female *and* found her half-way attractive at the same time.

But that was the thing: the attraction part was a stretch. It's not that Kate wasn't cute — even pretty or beautiful. It's that I wasn't particularly attracted to her on a superficial level.

We had initially connected by (what she called) "nerding out" on the topic of teaching history — ancient Greek history to be exact. It wasn't my forte, antiquity, but I had just read a few books about it and she was about to teach the subject to her 5th graders. So we talked about talking about the ancient Greeks at some undetermined point in the future. Then we exchanged phone numbers.

The problem was that I was first intrigued by our mutual interest in Greek history; second, by the fact that she seemed intellectually stimulating. The other thing was that she looked kind of cute too. Yes, the initial attraction was less than magnetic, which is probably why I hesitated on calling her back. In fact, my hesitation lasted about a week, until I felt somewhat guilty and mustered enough interest to call her and set a date. Except it wasn't a real date. I only suggested that we extend our "dorky" conversation about Socrates at a coffee shop.

I didn't think about nor prepare much that evening before arriving at the café to meet Kate. I only remember sitting down and watching her enter, looking much more fashionable and well dressed than me. She was wearing a long, flowing summer dress and rustic silver jewelry that shined when the light hit it just right. I began by sharing two books with her that had been collecting dust in the back seat of my car. One was a general history titled *Antiquity* and the other was the classic play *Antigone* by Sophocles. Her facial expression read disappointment. I suspected she was surprised that I really did want to discuss her upcoming lesson topic; that it wasn't just an excuse to meet her again.

As fate — or Kate — would have it, a rather loud and annoying open mic commenced about ten minutes into our coffee shop conversation. We both agreed that the performers were too distracting and too amateur. That's when she suggested we grab a beer around the corner at a bar, and I agreed.

After the first drink, we had a second — then a third. She asked me so many questions about my life and work, and expressed so much interest in me, that I felt I had to reciprocate with questions about her life as well. Before I knew it I was drunk, and so was she, and we were getting along even better. At that point her cuteness had turned into beauty and my judgment turned to mush. Kate — who I assumed knew her intentions all along (and was following her learned quasi-feminist impulses of *Sex in the City*) put the moves on me. She was on a mission. And I didn't complain. I'd always found it difficult — especially while drinking alcohol — to resist the advances of an aggressive female who was at least somewhat attractive.

And that was it — not very romantic. But it somehow turned into love over time. Real love. I guess that's what happens when you meet someone like Kate, who is talented at subtly controlling things on the sly. I guess people like that get what they want a lot, regardless if things were really meant to unfold in such a way. That night, unbeknownst to me, Kate had begun to orchestrate us into a three-year relationship that might have never been — or might not have been meant to be — but had brought us all the way to *the big question...*

"Can I help you young man?" said the gray-haired lady working the gift shop counter.

"Uh, yeah." I said, emerging from my memory reel. It took a second to remember what my immediate question was; to remember why I was standing in the middle of the mission gift shop on a weekday morning.

"How familiar are you with public transportation?" I asked.

With that single inquiry, the gift shop lady lit up. She told me she rode the bus everyday. So I asked her about the best way to Pacific Beach: "By bus or trolley?" She confidently told me the bus. In fact, she insisted on the bus. She told me to turn right at the bottom of the stairs, head west down Friars road, and catch the bus in front of the stadium.

"Short walk. Much faster," she assured me, "than taking the trolley to Old Town and transferring again. Oh gosh yes." Clearly, she knew the system better than I did.

I descended the stairs to the sidewalk and continued West, toward the dense mass of towering concrete known as Qualcomm Stadium. I remembered the Padres used to play baseball games there when I was a kid. I liked baseball back then.

And it occurred to me that San Diego's professional baseball team was named after Spanish priests — some of whom enslaved and forced assimilation on the Kumeyaay Indians. And I used to happily cheer that team on with my dad and my friends, without ever giving it a thought.

Go Padres!

Profession

I suppose I have a right to be disturbed by historical omissions and contradictions. After all, I'm a history professor — or at least I was.

It was once my dream job. My desire to become a professor of history started when I went to college and realized that most of what I had been taught about the past was either false or missing significant chunks of information. At that point I became somewhat obsessed with learning about hidden truths in history, and my obsession pushed me all the way through graduate school.

However, having a position as an adjunct history professor wasn't as romantic or rewarding as I had once imagined. It sounded respected and dignified to some, but that was about the extent of it.

My first day on the job I was mistakenly called "Doctor Rodriquez" by one of my students. I had to correct her. I only had a Master's degree. And I quickly came to find out that being an adjunct professor had little to no respect or dignity attached to the title. "Adjunct" was just a fancy way for saying "part-time." It meant that I got paid by the hour — good at seventy dollars an hour; bad if the department only offered about six hours a week. Good if you liked health benefits. Bad if you liked any sense of job security and stability. Bad if you didn't like driving across town all day and night to almost every community college in the county, just to make ends meet.

And occasionally bad if you're susceptible to being distracted by attractive college girls. *Did you know most of the women in Playboy magazine are of college-age?* But honestly, that aspect was only distracting from time to time. Because only once every year or two would I have a student who looked like an international bikini model *and* had an ounce of self-confidence and maturity. It was this kind of rare distraction that would make me momentarily forget the most basic facts, like what General Sherman did in Georgia at the end of the Civil War, or where Martin Luther King was when he was shot, or what year America entered World War I. It made me drift and daydream and forget that I was probably fifteen years older than these young women. I would go blank for a couple seconds and then be rushed back into reality as forty silent students stared and wondered what the hell was going through my little, adjunct mind.

Good thing my thoughts weren't transparent. Good thing I had Kate as my girlfriend, I thought. She was solid—stable and consistent. She kept me grounded in reality—as much as I tried to avoid it sometimes. I figured studying and teaching the brutal truth about history was more than enough reality for one human being to absorb.

Qualcomm Stadium still bobbed to the left of me as I hoofed my way west toward the next bus stop. The stadium was surrounded by an asphalt sea of empty parking spaces, covered with dark oil stains. The stadium was built before the Qualcomm corporation even existed. Before that, the event center was called Jack Murphy Stadium—named after a popular San Diego sports writer. Naming a stadium after a sports writer made sense to me. However, naming a stadium after a communications technology company made much less sense. Then again, after studying history for over a decade, most things didn't make much sense to me anymore. And it made me wonder if I'd chosen the wrong profession.

But for a long while, my career and my relationship with Kate all seemed to make sense — going by unquestioned. In a word, I was complacent.

Confession

The "short walk" turned out to be longer than I anticipated, and the solitude gave me more time than usual to ruminate. Or maybe it was that I didn't have a cell phone to distract me.

My brief detour to the mission got me thinking that the same old priest who molested those kids and touched that unsuspecting woman (and told me that my non-church going family would go straight to hell) used to listen to my confessions as a Catholic schoolboy.

It was an archaic ritual we were subjected to: the sacrament of confession. In fact, I still feel guilty sometimes for absolutely no reason other than that I was indoctrinated at Immaculate Conception Catholic school during the most formative years of my life. And that—it seems—was the key to Catholicism: There's always something to feel guilty about (and fearful of). That's how they keep you in. That is, according to Kate, "Until you figure out their medieval mind tricks."

Every few months at Immaculate Conception, our teachers would line us up—little 3rd, 4th, 5th graders— single file, outside the high, imposing church walls. We would stand, knees locked, for up to an hour while every student, even the squeaky-clean honors students, reflected on the sins they would have to share with the priest. At the time we had no idea the old guy had a penchant for sinfulness of his own.

I remember one occasion very well. We were waiting in line outside the church for our turn to confess. I remember my stiff, light blue collared, uniform shirt. It was baggy enough for the sweat to roll all the way down my chest, from my neck to my waistline. And it was okay according to Miss Webb, our teacher, that we had to wait in line in the hot sun. Suffering was part of being Catholic. 3rd graders baking in the sun on a sweltering September day, forced to confess the evil acts they'd all committed, shouldn't dare complain about it. It was normal and necessary, she told us as she reclined in the shade.

That's when Paul, my blonde-haired friend who was sweating almost as much as me, turned around. He'd been standing in line just ahead of me. "Hey, Frank, what are you gonna' say?" he asked.

"I'm not sure. What about you?" I deflected.

"Well, I stole five bucks from my mom last week, but that's too bad to tell him," Paul explained. "I need a better one."

Paul was right. I thought about it for a moment. The reason why Paul didn't want the weight of his sin to be too heavy was because of the penance. First of all, "penance" shouldn't even be in the vocabulary of a 3rd grader. Penance was the punishment for your sins that the priest specified after you confessed. Our penance usually turned out to be kneeling on hard church kneelers while reciting countless prayers: typically a litany of Hail Marys' and Our Fathers.

"I'm gonna' go with the usual," I told Paul, as if I were a regular at the local pub.

"What's that?" he asked.

"Playboys," I said. "I'm gonna' tell him I sneaked and looked at my dad's Playboys and saw naked ladies and that that's wrong."

"Why 's that wrong?" Paul asked.

"I don't know," I said. "I just know it's not as bad as stealing."

"What about cussing?" he added.

"Oh, that's a good one too— not that bad, but true. I'll use both: cussing and Playboys," I said.

Cussing and Playboys it was. When it was my turn I entered the priest's low-lit, air-conditioned quarters and sat down on a plush, well-upholstered chair. The priest made the sign of the cross and then some other unfamiliar hand motion unique to members of his order. He sat at an angle so he was not directly facing me. He wore a velvet robe on top of his normal priest's costume. It was all very formal and Gothic and strange. Aside from the stained-glass windows and the ornate upholstery, the room felt like the apartment of a creepy, elderly chain-smoker.

He asked what I would like to confess. His voice was an intimidating baritone.

I told him about the cussing, then the Playboys.

He bowed his baldhead in disappointment, never looking directly at me. He confirmed that I had sinned. He confirmed that I was guilty and quoted a passage from the Bible, which implied that I would always be guilty — and that I might be sent to a burning inferno commonly known as HELL if I didn't turn my young life around and stop looking at pornography. He used foreboding words like "sacrilege" and "blasphemous" that I didn't really understand. Then he told me to enter the church, kneel

41

down, and say ten Hail Marys' and five Our Fathers, and everything would be okay.

Piece of cake, as I'd predicted.

I remembered passing by the row where penitent Paul was already kneeling in purgatory. I caught his attention and flashed both hands twice to indicate ten and five. He smiled and nodded, signaling that he was told the same. He gave me a thumbs up. I laughed but Miss Webb caught me. She scowled, rushed to my side, and walked me out of church by the ear. She scolded me into shame and told me I had 'earned' detention for the rest of the week.

I was busted.

But that priest—the one who liked to sexually molest women and children in his free time—never got busted. He never confessed either. He was transferred instead. I think he still works for the Church somewhere in a different diocese.

Yet I got busted quite a few times in Catholic school for much less serious offenses than sexual molestation. But I'm not so sure the penance and discipline did much to set me apart from all the other sinners out there. In many ways, I thought, it probably just delayed my exposure to real life.

I continued my walk along the hot, barren, concrete road, keeping an eye out for the next bus stop.

Illiteracy

Being a teacher, I've learned there are many different kinds of intelligence, and that they're not always interchangeable. For instance, a student could be good with math, but have a difficult time learning to read. Personally, I could read — history and literature — fairly well. But I discovered that day that I couldn't read a bus schedule to save my life.

I was bus schedule illiterate.

As I tried to read the schedule at the bus stop near Qualcomm Stadium, I couldn't make sense of the numbers. I'd never seen such a grid before, and the acronyms were all foreign to me. There were no other humans in sight, nobody to ask for help. *Was this the stop the gift shop lady was talking about?*

After waiting a few minutes and never seeing a bus, I kept on walking west on Friars Road. By that time, I was baking. The sun was gaining strength and beating down on my neck. I had forgotten to put sunscreen there. Over the years I had become preoccupied about religiously putting sunblock on my nose, but not anywhere else. My Roman nose, with a long, flat bridge, acted as a solar panel on occasion — angled to get the most of the sun's rays.

So, as I walked, I dug in my bag for the sunscreen. I first applied the lotion all over my neck, then re-applied it to my nose. I couldn't help it. The ironic thing was that my nose was regularly protected by more SPF's than humanly possible — which meant I'd probably end up getting skin cancer on my forehead or ears. I always forgot those spots.

I put the sunscreen in my backpack without breaking stride. That was about as successful with multi-tasking as I got. Kate always made fun of my inability to multi-task. And she was right: I couldn't handle it.

My feet began to feel the distance and the unforgiving ground as I continued on what seemed to be a Sahara of cement and gravel. I passed no pedestrians on the sidewalk and saw few signs of life until I finally passed the stadium parking lot and came upon a grand strip mall. It was brand new and had no character — like most things in Mission Valley — and imposed a surreal lens on the once undeveloped landscape.

The oversized strip mall seemed to be an island oasis of consumerism. It looked plastic and huge and stupid to me. Maybe it was because I had no money to buy groceries or furniture or hardware; or maybe because I had no house to put the furniture in, or fix up with the latest accessories. Even the cars passing by started to look like lifeless automatons rather than human operated vehicles. Since leaving the mission a few cars had blown by me, but now there was regular traffic, and the cars were much closer, moving in and out of the busy parking lot.

Nobody was on foot, and with greater proximity to cars, I began to notice the faces of drivers. They were looking at me diminutively, as if their being in an automobile gave them a superior status. They looked at me as if I was a peon, a cretin — a vagrant with no real mobility. And it made me start to resent the superficial lifestyles of the rich and even that middle class segment who fancied themselves pre-rich. *Wait, didn't that include me?* Perhaps I just envied the fact that they had cars that day, and I didn't. I was bus illiterate and they probably were too, but they didn't need to worry about it.

Even though I was heading directly due west, I started to feel off course. I was on foot for Christsakes. The plan was off-kilter, and how much time had already been wasted?

I imagined I wouldn't be a very good soldier. I'd be an even worse general, I thought, not only with directions and planning and such, but also with ordering young men to go kill other young men. I'd thought about this war question before. One time Kate and I talked about it as we drove through Mission Valley.

"I couldn't do that," I told her. "No matter how brainwashed I'd become."

"Do what?" she asked. She might have been distracted by the traffic, or the song on the radio.

"Couldn't order young soldiers to go kill other young soldiers," I said. "Unless it was World War II, I guess, and my unit was hunting down Hitler, Goebbels, Goering, and the rest of the highest ranking Nazis."

I remember Kate rolling her eyes at me as if to say 'Grow up' or 'Pull your head out of your ass, Frank.' Maybe she was sick of my historical references. So she didn't respond to me, but changed the subject to more practical matters. "We need to get to *Bed, Bath, and Beyond* before it closes," she said. That's how it went.

I figured I'd walked a couple of miles since leaving the mission. After passing the Ikea-dominated, mega-mini-mall, I spotted a bus stop. It was in the distance on the right side of the street with one woman sitting down on the bench. It had a sliver of artificial shade to sit under, and that alone was a great thing because beads of sweat had already started to form on my forehead. And I wanted a break. I also desperately needed someone to interpret the bus schedule.

As I made it closer to the stop, I noticed that the lone woman was older, probably around sixty, and definitely Asian. She was wearing dark slacks and cheap pink plastic sandals. Her black blouse looked silky and Oriental, with embroidered flowers on the collar. I passed in front of her as I approached the posted schedule.

"Hello," I said.

No response. But I was sure I had spoken loud enough for her to hear me. In reaction to the awkward silence, I returned my attention to the bus schedule. Again, it made no sense. My bus schedule illiteracy was really beginning to frustrate me. I had to ask her.

"Excuse me," I said, "Do you know what bus I should take to get to Pacific Beach?"

"Why you nee go beach?" she snapped with a nearly incomprehensible accent. Her tone seemed aggressive, but oddly enough she was smiling at me. *Was she really asking me to explain why I was going to my destination?*

"Um, my car is there. I just need the bus that goes directly west… to the beach," I said.

"Wes to beach… yo car — you no car?" she rattled out, in rapid staccato style. She was hard to understand, but I tried to attune my ears.

"My car is at beach. I need to pick up," I said, idiotically dropping the article 'the' and the pronoun 'it' as if worsening my own English would make me better understood.

46

"You re-tar or wha?" she asked.

Did she just ask me if I was a retard? I couldn't understand half the words coming out of her mouth. *Retard? –Really?* I didn't want to assume too much though. I didn't want to argue. I didn't want to be culturally insensitive either. And I needed her bus knowledge. Though her speech was a bit harsh and snappy, she always smiled after speaking.

"Where you go-ing?" She asked more clearly.

"To the beach," I repeated.

"Oh, beach—number 6—my bus too," she said.

"You're sure this bus goes West?" I pointed west, " — to the beach?" I felt the need to clarify and use clear hand motions.

"Yes, Wesss to beach. Wes to beach," she said, then smiled again, as if on cue.

When the bus arrived, she stood up and turned to me.

"You no know bus, do you?" she said. In a weird way, beneath the harsh broken English, she seemed to care about my well being.

"My first time," I said and half smiled like a freshman on day one of class.

"You bus vur-gen," she said and giggled.

I laughed. At least she had a sense of humor, I thought. And I was starting to understand more and more of her broken English. I also reminded myself that while her English was crappy, I had no clue how to speak her language—or any second language. And I didn't even have a decent hint at what her language might be:

47

Chinese, Vietnamese, Thai? In more ways than one, I was the ignorant one, not her.

She stepped onto the bus first. She showed her pass, and then turned back to me—standing awkwardly next to the bus driver—before she chose a seat near the front. The bus driver lowered his double chin into his neck and widened his eyes at me as if to say, 'What are you waiting for dumbass?'

"Ticket?" he barked.

"Buy day pass," the Asian woman interjected, "Five dollah all day. Bus and Trolley. Betta fuh you. Ride all day."

And for some reason I trusted her, so that's exactly what I did.

Miss Saigon

I was momentarily thankful I had met a helpful person and was in a motor-powered vehicle, moving at about fifty miles per hour. Though I had no idea what time it was, I hoped being on a direct bus would make up for my temporary derailing.

I sat in an aisle seat across from where the Asian woman sat upright with her hands rested on her knees. We were the only people on board aside from a few scattered transients in the back. I examined the wrinkles on her face from across the aisle. The ones on her forehead and by her eyes were deep and distinguished, but the sag lines around her mouth made her look like a bitter old fish. Sensing my curious stare, she turned to me and smiled, but without exposing her teeth or gums. She seemed nice enough despite the 'retard' comment — if that's what it was. And I figured I might as well find out what language her accent came from.

"Excuse me, I was just wondering: Where are you from?" I asked.

"Neea hoo-vah," she said.

It didn't sound like any Asian country or city I'd ever heard of: Nea-Hoo-Vah?

"Near hoo-vah. Hoo-vah hi schoo," she repeated.

Ohhh, Hoover High School, I thought and nodded. She lived near Hoover High. That was only a few miles from my parents' house.

"I meant what country are you from—originally?" I clarified.

"Aaah," she said, "Viet Nam."

She smiled, but only for a moment. I noticed the dramatic contrast between her animated smiles and her saggy fish mouth.

"Wow," I said.

"I leave Saigon 1976," she said. "Come to San Diego with husband and two kids."

I nodded, encouraging her to continue.

"Star new life here," she said. "Some-time pee-poh have to star over."

Coincidence, I thought, that she started her second life the same year I began my first—the year I was born. By that measure, I *was* still on my first, because I had never lived anywhere else or made such a drastic move.

The bus exited Friars Road, slowed, and made a big, gravity-testing left turn, south onto Texas Street. I looked ahead to the driver and then back at Miss Saigon (my slightly inappropriate name for her). I noticed we were no longer going west, but heading straight into the multi-mall shopper's paradise that was Mission Valley.

"Are you sure this bus goes to the beach?" I asked her for the second time. My initial doubts about our language barrier were re-emerging.

"Yes, beach!" she assured me.

"Are we gonna' get on the freeway then?"

I only asked because the freeway ran east and west, but if we didn't get on it, then we'd be forced to head south toward Normal Heights and downtown. There would be no logical westward road to head back toward the beach, unless this bus did a grand loop around the entire city. It was possible, I guessed. *What did I know about bus travel? Was I being a backseat-driving rookie?* Still it seemed wrong. I must have been wearing that doubtful sentiment on my face because Miss Saigon seemed annoyed that I didn't trust her wholeheartedly.

"Yes free-way, of cuss free-way!" she snapped. She didn't smile afterward. Her mouth just went flat. Then she quickly changed the subject. "You look like Ah-mer-can G.I. boxey from village ne-ah Saigon."

Was she associating me with the American soldiers who occupied her country for fifteen years and killed millions (yes, millions) of Vietnamese people? I didn't want to be connected with that—not even remotely. My brow lowered with concern.

"Boxey same as doctor," she explained. "Medic. Boxey help family and me. You look like boxey with—." She stroked her jaw and chin, referring to my beard. "Ha-ha. You look like boxey!"

I grinned, mostly in recognition that I had no idea what her association with me and the boxey meant, if it meant anything at all. My movie-driven mind conjured clips from the melodramatic, violent war films I'd watched as a kid— the parts where the lost platoon comes across a lone Vietnamese woman; the Americans yelling and cussing—

assuming she's the enemy. Maybe thinking about raping her.

What was going through Miss Siagon's head as she sat there on the bus, pondering those war years, and the boxey's face? — and my face! How had he helped her? What horrible things had she been subjected to? I wondered about these things as I watched her distant eyes and subtle facial cues. Then she pulled a serene smile, appearing to drift back to the present.

Miss Saigon continued, "Only thing diff-rent—he black and you white!" And she cackled out loud for a few seconds. "But same bee-ah, and smile… and way."

What? I reminded her of a black guy in Vietnam? And had she just called me 'white'? I overcorrected her as I'd been compelled to do a few times since I'd been mislabeled back in the 4th grade.

"I'm Mexican though."

"Ohhh," she said, "You look white."

I forced a polite grin. What was there to dispute? I *was* half white. But she, like many others, seemed to care less about my racial, categorical corrections. I didn't have a Mexican accent, or speak Spanish, or have skin that was a shade brown enough. Apparently, that's what most people needed to see and hear to authenticate my being "Mexican."

That I was *both* seemed to make it too complicated for people—and even ended up confusing me sometimes. So I changed the subject back to a history other than mine— something I'd been curious about since I first taught students about the Vietnam War and realized (like 99% of my field) I knew only what I'd read in books.

"What did you think about the other American soldiers during the war?" I asked.

"I only know boxey. I only talk to boxey." She said. "Other G.I. burn and kill village next to mine. I don't like. I don't like. Buh I don't know dem."

This time she didn't smile when she finished speaking. Maybe I shouldn't have asked. She just shook her head for a second, effectively ending our conversation.

I returned my attention to the road because we were nearing the freeway, but the bus didn't turn onto it. *Jesus Christ!* We were heading south into Normal Heights and North Park, and who knew where next. This was clearly not the right bus — not the bus to the beach. When it came to directions, this Vietnamese lady didn't know what the hell she was talking about.

But there she sat, in solemn contemplation of the horrors she'd experienced in her homeland — at least that's what I assumed was on her mind. And I had brought it all up. How could I ask about our bus route without coming across as an insensitive bastard? But before I could ask my next frustrated bus question, Miss Saigon continued where she had left off:

"But American G.I. not bad, just pawn."

"Just pawn?" I said, surprised by her chess reference.

"Just pawn in war game... Poor pee-poh force to fight, force to go fight for re-tar Ameh-ican gov-ment."

So she *did* call me a retard earlier, that was confirmed: same word, different context, clear meaning. And though she may not have been the most politically correct, her interpretation rang true.

"Just like gov-ment now. Retar. Bush retar. Obama retar. No change fo beh-tah... Do same pol-see like Vietnam, only more control media now. More control pee-poh puh-spective too," she said.

I nodded again. She had insightful points through her thick accent. She had first-hand experience too. Her imperfect pronunciation and broken English became less distracting as her intelligence became more and more apparent with the message of every sentence. But as profound and relevant as her comments were, I was much more concerned with the fact that our bus was heading south — in the wrong direction.

I needed to get my car back and I needed to meet Kate, who I was still referring to as my girlfriend.

I pictured myself telling Kate about Miss Saigon later that night. I wondered if she would be amused, interested, or only suspicious that I was talking to a female for so long without her knowledge. Kate wasn't a jealous person, really. In fact, she was quite secure with herself and independent. However, over the past months she had become more susceptible to jealousy.

I supposed I had lived in San Diego for too long and knew too many women who she had never met. Occasionally we ran into them. They were usually old friends or acquaintances, but something about their mere existence seemed to disturb her. I only knew this because I had noticed little signs. I could tell Kate had checked my phone once or twice to see who'd called or sent me messages. She also checked the history on my laptop a few times "by accident," she said. Up until then, I had never checked my own history on my computer, so I tried it and realized this: It was no accident.

I imagined Kate meeting Miss Saigon right after hearing about her. After Kate's first whiff of suspicion, I could witness her shock from being wrong about the nature of our conversation. *Would that finally make her trust me? Could anything?* I had never given Kate a solid reason not to trust me. Unless she could sense that I had been growing indifferent, becoming more and more bored out of my mind. Or was it that I hadn't proposed to her after almost three years? — *No, she had never directly said a word about that.*

I quit staring out the bus window and returned my attention to my Vietnamese acquaintance. If only I could communicate clearly with Miss Saigon, I thought. If only Miss Saigon had given me the correct bus information. *Was there any use in inquiring further?* I could have asked again or complained about her giving me the wrong directions, but what would be the point? I decided to go speak with the bus driver. But before I stood up Miss Saigon chimed in with a new topic.

"You have girl-friend o wife… o gay man?"

"Where does this bus go?" I asked, ignoring her unrelated question.

"You like gay man?" she said.

"No, I have girlfriend!" I said, somewhat defensively.

She had a true knack for neglecting tact and adding rude comments.

"You tell true o lie?" she said, clearly toying with me.

"I like women, sorry to disappoint you." I tried to minimize any homophobia in my tone.

"Oh, you have girlfriend?" she asked.

"Yes," I said.

It was a lie. *Or was it?* The question hadn't been put to me that directly by anyone in the past four weeks. And I felt that Kate still *was* my girlfriend. *We were probably just taking a break. We were in a brief period of limbo before getting back together. It had happened before.* But I didn't want to get into it. What did a little lie matter anyway? This old Vietnamese woman had probably lied to me too. Our bus wasn't going to the beach and she knew it.

"Where does—" I started but was interrupted.

"—This bus go downtown, but go beach too!" she insisted.

She smiled again. Unlike me, she looked unaffected.

Then the bus turned left onto University, which had us going east—the opposite direction. I looked at Miss Saigon in a mixture of despair and anger, but it quickly turned into reluctant acceptance that I was indeed off course.

"You okay, boxey. Dey turn south on 30 stree, then to beach," she said.

As if she had amused herself enough at my expense, Miss Saigon grabbed her bags, secured them in her arms, and stood up. She leaned on the seat in front of her and pulled the white cord running along the window. I noticed its function for the first time. Pulling on it seemed to indicate that one needed to get off. I was learning.

"Where are you going?" I asked. It came out desperately, as if she was suddenly my only guide and without her I'd be lost in the darkness of the San Diego bus system. Or maybe I felt she had led me astray and wanted her to guarantee I'd be back on the right track.

"I get off now, boxey," she told me.

Did she just call me "boxey" again? I guess I'd already made up a name for her too.

"But you stay on bus," she added. "You go all way to beeeech—then figuh it out."

With those final, annoying words Miss Saigon departed. Although I had grown exasperated with her, the bus seemed to have a strange void without her. And I didn't even know her real name.

Break Down

Not long after Miss Saigon left me, somewhere between North Park and South Park on 30th street, the bus jolted forward and died. It felt like the bus driver down shifted and released the clutch too soon. He tried the ignition and stick shift as we rolled forward with no engine, then pulled to the side of the road. He turned the ignition a few more times. Nothing.

In short order the bus driver stood up, turned to the passengers and said, "Sorry, folks. This one's down for now." Then he walked onto the sidewalk, pulled out his cell phone, lit a cigarette, and made a call. A few passengers sighed and groaned.

As I sat there, on a stationary bus, with a rare sense of dejection and lack of direction in my own hometown, I tried to note the positives: I was alive and healthy. I could walk and talk and function well. I was relatively young too. I didn't grow up in a war-torn country like Vietnam. And at the very least, I had an all-day bus/trolley pass and plenty of time left to get to my car and meet up with Kate.

Did she even get my text though? Would she ever want to talk to me or see me again?

The abandoned passengers sitting and standing around me, no more than a dozen people in all, expressed their displeasure—hemming and hawing. Then, one by one, they all started to get off the bus. I was just waiting for cues when I made eye contact with an older black woman who remained in her seat.

I asked her: "Excuse me, but what happens now?"

She looked at me like I was the dumbest person on the planet. Right after she rolled her eyes, she said, "They're sending someone to fix the bus and bring a replacement."

"Oh," I said, "How long does that take?"

"Thirty minutes. Sometimes longer," she said.

"Thanks," I said.

There were a handful of people waiting on the sidewalk and some others were already walking away. If I was to put any faith in what Miss Saigon had told me about the ultimate destination of the bus, then I could safely step off, walk south down 30th for a while, and hop on the same line thirty minutes later. Even if Miss Saigon was totally wrong — which she probably was — any bus heading south on 30th would surely go downtown and I could get moving in the right direction from there.

Just to be sure, I attempted to check with the cell phone-engrossed bus driver as I exited through the front door. I saw a quick flash of my semi-lost bearded self in the reflection of his aviator sunglasses. Though I spoke and waved to get his attention, he didn't acknowledge my existence whatsoever. He was busy taking a break. And he was on the phone, like almost everyone else standing there next to that dead city bus.

High School Confessional

While traversing Switzer Canyon on 30th street, the strong and familiar scent of imported eucalyptus swept into my nostrils. There was an occasional passing car, but no other signs of life on the road. My attention was drawn to the canyon below, and when I noticed a tent in an inconspicuous spot in the bushes, it made me think of homeless, illegal immigrants — and one of the most shameful moments of my life.

It happened back when I was a sophomore in high school. It was about ten o'clock on a weekend night in suburban and serene Scripps Ranch. I was standing in front of a 7-11 with two friends, Jared and Mike. We had just finished playing *Street Fighter* for the 20th time, which reminded us of the sobering fact that we didn't have cars, the ability to drive them or, more importantly, anywhere to go. As we came to grips with the limitations of being fifteen and hanging out in a strip mall, a Ford truck pulled up with some familiar faces in it. It was Anthony, Houston, and another guy I recognized but couldn't name. All three were popular, football-playing seniors from our high school. I wasn't sure they had ever noticed our existence before that night.

"You guys got anything goin' on tonight?" asked Houston with a tone of authority. He was the oldest-looking one of them, a weightlifter with enough muscle mass and acne to suggest beginner steroid use.

"Just cruising around," said my friend Jared, giving the appropriate if inaccurate answer.

"Well, we were just gonna' get some brewskies. You can pitch in cash if you guys wanna' join us," said Anthony, extending a surprising invitation.

We scrounged around in our pockets and came up with a few dollars between us. Jared handed it over. I think we were offering our money more out of interest in hanging out with upperclassmen than out of any burning desire to consume alcohol.

Soon after Houston bought the beers, we were screeching around residential corners and holding on to the sides of the truck bed for dear life. Anthony was the lone senior in the open truck bed with Jared, Mike, and I. He did most of the talking because we were all a bit intimidated that these guys were bigger and older than us. Of course, they were also cooler than us by default, just based on their senior status — if you believed that kind of thing. And back then, we did.

I didn't pay much attention to where we were going until I realized we were out of suburbia and on a dark, dirt road, far from any houses. The road kept getting progressively bumpier, and less and less appealing as a hang out spot. *Did we really have to drive this far off the grid just to drink a few beers?*

Jared finally asked Anthony, "Hey, do you know where we're going, man?"

No immediate answer. Anthony looked through the rear window at the back of Houston's shaved, military-style head. He turned back to us and said unenthusiastically, "It's his idea."

What was his idea?

The truck skidded to an abrupt stop in the dirt road. I had to brace myself from sliding and hitting my head on the back window. I remember the edge I had to grab onto to brace myself was ice cold and damp, and it reminded me that I was far from my home neighborhood.

Houston stepped out of the car. He stuck his thick neck in the doorway to grab something from behind the front seat. When he emerged he had two baseball bats under his right arm, a police-officer-style mag flashlight under his left, and a crow bar in his hand.

He smiled and said, in a devilish tone, "Let's go get some dirty Mexicans."

The guy who was riding shotgun laughed out loud at Houston's blunt comment, but the rest of us stood silently. Houston handed his friends the weapons, and kept the crow bar and flashlight for himself.

"Well, come on," he commanded, "The sophomores can carry the beers."

We all obediently followed him into the darkness of the canyon. Only his flashlight gave a hint of where the trail was heading. I couldn't believe it. I was with a group of Mexican immigrant bashers and I was Mexican! —Half or whatever, it didn't matter.

I had heard about this kind of thing on the news a few times. Neo-Nazi type guys would arm themselves and go in the canyons of San Diego where they had heard newly arrived immigrants were camping. When they found their shanties they would viciously attack unsuspecting immigrants. Some of the self-proclaimed militia men killed innocent men and whole families. And there I was, walking with privileged Catholic school white boys who planned to do the same thing. Would I end up on the 11 o'clock news as part of this group of racist, teenage vigilantes — murderers!? Or would I become one of the victims?

I turned to my good friend Jared.

"Is he serious?" I asked in a low voice.

Jared didn't say a word. He just gave me that look that said he was more frightened to *not* do what Houston said.

"Jesus Christ," I whispered to Mike. He didn't respond.

As we moved deeper into the canyon, I felt my soul sinking. I approached Anthony, who was a few paces ahead of me. I thought quickly about what I could say to him that might change our fatal course.

"Hey, man, aren't you Mexican?" I asked him.

"No, I'm Portuguese" he said, with an expression that was straight and hard to read. I prayed Anthony would stand up to his peers, but it didn't look promising.

Were all of these guys thoughtless, violent, xenophobes who actually thought they were doing something good? *I couldn't keep going. I couldn't.* If we came upon a small migrant camp around the corner it would be too late, I thought. Dumb group psychology, irrational fear, teenage peer pressure — and that tool Houston as the ring leader — would catapult us into assault and maybe even murder before anyone had a chance to stop it. Even if Houston or all of these guys — my friends included — decided to jump me or beat me to death with their aluminum bats, I couldn't go any further.

I stopped in the middle of the road...

They kept moving for a few seconds, until it was obvious I had abandoned the herd. That last scratching sound of Houston's shoes against the loose dirt ushered in a terrorizing silence for a few long seconds.

"What the hell are you doing?" he said with his flashlight pointed at me, trying to keep his voice down. It was more of a hushed yell. I didn't move or say a word in response. I was too scared. Houston walked back toward me. Each of his steps made a crunching sound on the rocky dirt road.

"I'm not gonna do this." I said, my voice cracking with fear.

There was silence. They all looked at Houston. I could tell they feared for my life and had no idea where my courage was coming from. It might have been from my dad, or at least the thought of my dad knowing what I was about to be a part of. Yes, maybe I simply feared the family disgrace more than Houston beating me to a bloody pulp.

He paused and then laughed for a second, turning and looking at some of the guys and then back at me.

"You're not Mexican, Frank," Houston said.

"Yes, I am." I told him. "And my name is actually Francisco."

At that Houston cackled maniacally until he remembered he was trying to be quiet so those faceless Mexicans he planned on hunting down wouldn't hear us coming. Houston's beady eyes were impossible to read. He could have very well nailed me with that crow bar held in his right hand, and then bludgeoned me to death with the other end of the flashlight.

"Hey, you used to play football, didn't you?" Houston asked me, which was the strangest non sequitur I'd ever heard in my life.

"Yeah, for one year," I said.

"Why'd you quit?"

Why on earth was he asking? What synapses were disconnected in this guy's warped brain? How'd he, of all seniors, become so popular?

After thinking about it for a moment I said: "Because it wasn't fun anymore." I was beginning to think he might be clinically insane but had yet to be diagnosed.

"Well, you were good," he said. "You shoulda' stuck with it, man." Then he chuckled to himself, like a mafia goon. "I thought you were Portuguese too."

"No." I said.

No – but would it matter anyway? I probably looked very scared and confused to him – that is, if someone like him was even capable of picking up on facial expressions. I kind of doubted it.

In what seemed like slow motion, Houston held up the crow bar over his head and turned to the rest of the guys. I guessed he was either going to kill me, or give a speech to his followers about the prudence of immigrant bashing. He did neither.

"Guys," he said, "I think we should go back and drink those beers before they get warm."

We all jumped back in the truck and didn't mention a word about what had just happened. In fact, I never told anyone what had happened that night, until now…

And I only wish I could say that that was the truth. But sometimes it's hard to tell the whole truth — the shameful truth.

Here's the truth:

That night when Houston was prepared to lead a group of upper-middle-class teenagers to go beat the brains out of some poor Mexicans camping in Penasquitos Canyon, I didn't stand up to him the way I just described. I didn't have the courage I wished I had. I didn't stand there and tell him to kill me because I was Mexican too.

You know what I *really* did?

I secretly begged Anthony, his senior friend who seemed reasonable enough, to convince Houston to stop searching for brown people to attack and, instead, just go drink the beers somewhere else while they were still cold. And it worked.

I didn't bravely come to a halt as an individual act of defiance and confront Houston, even though part of me regrets it now and wished I had — so much so that I'd wanted to tell it that way.

But Houston really did ask me those unexpected, misplaced questions about my brief football career. In fact, everything else I described about that night actually happened, except for the part where I was courageous and took a stand and risked my life by saying I was Mexican.

You know why I didn't do that?

Because I was scared shitless back then.

66

The Station

After walking down 30th long enough to get lost in a memory, a #6 bus marked "Downtown" pushed a draft of wind across the left side of my face, and then stopped a block ahead of me. I started to jog to catch it, but before I made it past two driveways the bus was on the move again. My disappointment was minimal, however — mostly because I had lowered my San Diego public transit expectations to just about nothing. I started to think about turning up a random street, any street, as long as it headed west. *Would getting to Pacific Beach directly on foot be faster and more of an accomplishment than figuring out the goddamn bus schedule?*

I heard my stomach growling and realized I had only eaten a small bowl of cereal all day. Soon I was at an intersection that showed some signs of commercial life — or at least a few eating options. But one place looked too pricey; the other plain and unappealing. In the distance I spotted a Roberto's taco shop, which seemed to be the best option. I had limited funds. But as I neared the familiar red and yellow sombrero logo, I was reminded that I had eaten Mexican food for every meal the day before; and the day before that. I could've easily inhaled another bean and cheese burrito or rolled tacos, but my stomach might not have appreciated it.

Across the street I noticed a uniquely built, open-air patio. It was a new place: The Station. I remembered reading about it in the local weekly. It was part of the gentrification of the area, but was supposed to be tasty and affordable. I stepped into the sparsely populated, renovated restaurant and seated myself at a high table by a window facing the street. I couldn't help but notice an ancient-looking wooden door leading to their patio. The door was at least eighty years old, which is considered ancient in San Diego.

There was a girl—young woman, I suppose—leaning over the bar as if she was checking out the thickly mustached bartender's shoes as they chatted. She looked twenty-something. I didn't really care what it was that they were talking about, or what was making her stand on her tip toes and lean over the bar like that. I was too busy admiring her seemingly practiced pose.

She was attractive, yes: olive colored skin, wavy dark hair; athletic yet feminine. She had a well-drawn tattoo on her calf and one on her thigh that ran a few inches farther up her skirt. It looked like a tiger or some sort of feline, but I wasn't sure from that distance. It could've been a cat woman—or a devil with paws and a tail—but it was partly covered by the bottom of her black skirt. I didn't particularly like tattoos, but thought they were sexy if done tastefully. This girl was definitely tasteful and sexy. She was an ethnic mixture of something, but I couldn't tell what. Whatever it was, it was good. She turned and approached my table, eyes sparkling.

"Hello there, how are you?"

She asked me with sass, as if she was a stripper—not a waitress about to take my order.

"Good," I said, with a smile that conceded my lack of creativity by giving her the most standard, meaningless response.

"I like your beard." She said.

Her smile seemed warm and flirtatious. Was she flirting or just being a nice waitress? It was hard to tell.

"Thanks," I said, "It takes a lot of hard work to get it to this point."

'It took many lazy days of avoiding a shave to get this mangy beard,' I should have added — anything to make her laugh. But she didn't. She just smirked, never letting her eyes drift from mine.

"Are you in a band?" She asked, out of nowhere.

"Nope," I said.

"Oh, it must be the beard," she said. "A lot of guys in bands around here with big, scruffy beards."

I didn't say thanks. I didn't know what to say to that. It wasn't really a compliment. It was as though she was momentarily interested in me because she presumed I might be a local rock star, but could care less otherwise. I nodded with a dumb smile on my face, and she smirked at me and walked away. *I may have ruined a perfectly good flirtatious moment. I had zero game, I knew it.*

I returned my attention to the ancient door next to the bar. I had read about it once. It was the original door to the old 30th street trolley station that once stood at that exact same spot. The wood, recently painted over but still faded, had big cracks that made it look antique and Western. The metal crank with the wheel handle gave it more authenticity, though it was purely decorative.

It turns out that back in the 1920's, San Diego had an extensive light rail system that worked its way down 30th and through the city quite efficiently. But when cars started to get in the way in the 1950's and became a much more profitable enterprise — from manufacturing to retail to gas sales — the old trolleys were removed. A similar thing happened in Los Angeles. Gridlock traffic was preferred by those who stood to profit the most. The new trolley system that resurfaced in San Diego a couple decades ago consisted of only three lines: two that moved east and west, and one that went north and south. Its coverage was spotty at best.

Too bad the old trolley system was gone, I thought. It made me want to go back in time. Unfortunately, the reincarnation of *The Station* I was sitting in no longer provided cheap, clean, efficient public transportation. Just organic burgers, veggieburgers and drinks.

"Let me guess, you wanna" burger?" the waitress asked, having suddenly reappeared, her interest rejuvenated.

Maybe she'd thought about my potential on the way back to the kitchen and the non-musician thing didn't matter anymore. Perhaps she wasn't even thinking about me or flirting with me and it was all in my imagination. Perhaps my flight of fancy with this hot waitress, along with my historical tangents, was just keeping me distracted from myself — and *Kate*.

"Yes," I said, "I'll take the veggie burger with bacon and cheese."

The waitress looked up from her note pad and grinned at me. She seemed to appreciate the ease with which I contradicted myself.

"Not a Veggie or a Vegan, I take it?" she said.

"I have no idea what 'Vegan' means," I said, even though I had a vague idea.

She giggled.

"I'm Natasha," she said. "What's you're name?"

"Frank."

"Ooh, 'Frank'. Very exotic," she joked.

I smiled and nodded in acknowledgment of my common, irreversible name. *Were we flirting again – or was I being presumptuous?*

"Do you want a beer?" She asked.

"No thanks, " I said.

"It's on the house." She winked.

"Okay," I said. I usually didn't drink so early in the day, but this was a gift. Maybe I wasn't being presumptuous about her after all.

When Natasha returned with my amber-colored beer, at the risk of losing any cool points I might have had, and bypassing the more trendy, bullshit conversation piece about the type of microbrew she was handing me, I asked about the ancient door and the history of *The Station*. And she knew the whole story! She actually seemed interested about history for a few seconds, which excited me. I listened and nodded and added a few details I thought I knew before a rude condiment request from the outside patio drove her away.

While I waited, I sat there and peered at the cracks in the ancient door, then out the window at the tree lined street. I pictured San Diego in the late 1920's, the station, the trolley rolling by, a whistling sound, passengers in black top hats getting on and off, the undeveloped spaces on the way to Balboa Park, the old Navy boys roaming the street.

I pictured myself walking into a local San Diego restaurant back then. The restaurant had a sign on the front window that said "No colored, no Mexicans, no Japs." I would have grabbed that sign and thrown it on the floor in front of the owners and called them "Goddamn racists." Then I would have ran away. *Was I afraid that my white great grandparents would have been those racist shop owners? Or my Mexican great grandparents the victims?*

Long ago there really was a San Diego restaurant with a sign on the front window that said "No colored, no Mexicans, no Japs." I saw it in a black and white picture at a local museum on a school field trip in junior high. And I only remember one other thing from that field trip: Our teacher told us that racism was only a problem in the South.

Finally, my veggie bacon cheeseburger arrived and I shifted my focus onto eating. I think the combination of Natasha and the history behind the ancient door had also made me forget about my hungry, shriveling stomach for a while — amongst other things.

After enjoying my burger, I jotted down some notes on a napkin — notes to map out the rest of my new, zig-zaggy route. My slightly altered plan looked like a primitive handwritten version of this: *bus to Downtown, trolley to Old Town, bus to PB*. I felt like I still had a decent amount of time, but I wasn't sure.

"Hey Natasha, what time is it?" I asked as she walked by my table. I said her name as if I was a regular who'd known her for years.

"What, are you in a hurry all of a sudden?" She asked.

"No... Well, yes," I said.

I paused. I explained to her that I was riding the bus for the first time and had been knocked off course a bit, and that I was on my way to PB, when she interrupted.

" — Pacific Beach!?" she asked, "What's *there*?" Her tone implied that Pacific Beach was the most culturally deprived, superficial, former frat-boy-filled place in San Diego. And it pretty much was.

"My car's there. I need to pick it up from the mechanic." I said.

"Gotcha." Then she inhaled deeply as if she had a mysterious idea to share. She peered at her only other table as they departed and said to me:

"You seem like you have a good eye."

"In what way?" I asked.

"In an artistic way."

"Ok. Thanks," I said.

I'd like to think so, but I wasn't sure I believed her. *Had she caught me staring at her earlier? Was she being sarcastic again?* I took it as a strange, undeserved compliment and had to ask:

"Why do you say that?"

"Because, ya' know, the history thing, this old door you've been looking at," she said. "I don't know, just the way you gaze at things. Seems like you're thinking a lot. Like you have an opinion."

"Oh," I said. "Thanks."

I hoped and assumed that most people were thinking and had opinions too, but if she wanted to compliment me on these basic points then I figured I'd gladly accept.

"I paint." she said, as if she was confident enough to publicly declare this to select people, yet too insecure to call herself an artist. "Well," she explained, "I do Dada-inspired stuff with paint and print collage, but with a historical twist."

I smiled and nodded and almost said "Cool" but didn't want to sound phony and unoriginal. I almost said "Awesome" but didn't want to sound like a dumbass.

"Rad." I said, which sounded dumb, dated, *and* phony as it came out.

"Can you look at some of my pieces?" she asked.

"Sure," I said.

"Great. Gimme a second."

She skipped away from my table and disappeared into the kitchen. *Did she keep her art in the back of the restaurant? Did she do this to everyone? How long was this gonna take?* She bounced back to my table with a purse hanging over her shoulder and a mixture of anxiety and excitement in her eyes.

"Ready to go?" she said.

"What? Where?" I asked.

"Oh, to my apartment. It's right around the corner," she said, as if I should've known.

"But—" I started.

"—You promised."

No I hadn't promised anything, I thought. Not even close. But she was so intriguing—beautiful—as she pleaded, with her head tilted playfully to one side. Her pose helped me notice part of a green and black tattoo peeking out on the tan skin around her collar.

"What about the check?" I asked. "And aren't you working?"

"Oh, I covered it and I'm off now. Don't worry about it." she said. "Ready?"

It was an obligatory trap. *How could I say no?* I'd agreed to see her artwork and she'd already paid for my lunch and a beer. Plus, she was becoming more and more attractive by the second. She must have been interested in me at some level, but it was still hard to see her angle. This girl, Natasha, was young, artistic, impulsive, and willing to take risks. I think I envied that about her and was instantly drawn in because of it.

Natasha

Her apartment really was around the corner, less than a block away. The yellow and white-trimmed, cracking paint of the wooden cottage made it look almost as old as the antique door in the restaurant. She led me inside her small, surprisingly dark apartment and directed me to sit down on an unkempt futon covered by a cheap cotton tapestry while she went to the bathroom.

I felt weird. Though I had only flirted and sat down in Natasha's apartment, I already felt guilty — guilty because I was old enough to know that I had put myself in a very precarious position. Guilty because I couldn't help but visualize Kate's face — her knowing eyes — because I still felt like I was her boyfriend. Perhaps Natasha was asking for an honest, objective opinion of her art and that was all. But that idea was sounding increasingly unlikely.

Natasha was doing something beyond flirting. She'd brought me to her house for Christsake. And now, as she was prepping in her bathroom, I was only one brush by, one lean in, one close whiff away from making out with this girl — and who knew where that would lead. Yeah, it was an exciting and fun thought. I was almost positive she would look gorgeous naked and I was curious about where those tattoos started and ended, but there was the guilt. *I had a girlfriend.* That thought had been embedded in me. And it was a serious relationship, at least at one point. *Kate hadn't responded to my texts or emails lately, but that was beside the point. What if our meeting that night went well?*

Either way, Kate would not have approved of me in Natasha's apartment. In fact, she would have blown up at the mere thought of that scene, even after being reminded that —

"Don't look."

I heard Natasha say it through the bathroom door with an intonation and timing that suggested the exact opposite. Then she opened the bathroom door and darted, half naked in her underwear, across the small nub of a hallway, through her bedroom door. She was a wild one. And she was torturing me now — it was clear.

"I'll be out in a second," she said.

I shook my head in disbelief as I checked out her framed pictures of serious debauchery and ephemeral friendship displayed in cheap frames on top of her bookshelf. I checked out her books — my habit when in a new residence — and recognized only Hemingway smashed in between more colorful contemporary bindings and female authors I'd never heard of before.

"Ready?" she asked from around the corner.

"Uh-huh." I said, uncertain if she would emerge with a large canvas painting or naked — or both.

"You like Hemingway?" I asked through the wall.

"Not really," she said, still in the other room. "He's pretty much a sexist, racist, chauvinist, pig."

"I won't argue with that," I said, "but have you read *For Whom the Bell Tolls*?

"Nope" she said.

"Well, I think in that book he gets it."

"Gets what?" she asked. Even through thin walls and a half-open door, her voice was clear.

"Love." I said.

I savored the simplicity of the one word response, but wondered if it sounded insightful or lame. She didn't answer, but I could hear that she stopped shuffling things around for a second, so I continued:

"If for only a moment, I think he gets love as the essence of life. You know, what love means and that its really the only meaning for us… human beings, that is."

I added "human beings" awkwardly at the end in order to make sure she didn't think I meant her and me. It was a leap, but who knew how fast she operated in that department? I mean, I *was* in her apartment already.

—And what the hell did I know about love anyway? Was I trying to impress her? Wasn't I repeating what someone else had told me about that book a long time ago? Was it an old girlfriend or a literature professor who'd said it? And how did I know if Hemingway "got it" if I didn't even "get it"?

"That's beautiful," she said, emerging from around the corner, hiding behind a five foot tall by three foot wide canvas.

I first noticed not the artwork but her lips pressed against the top of the unframed canvas. Her mouth and eyes expressed that she was even more interested and warmly suggestive than she had been at the restaurant.

"I probably heard that somewhere else," I admitted.

"Well, the way you said it was beautiful, Frank."

She called me Frank. The way she said my name was familiar. It was alluring. It was as if she planned on asking me what I thought of her art only as a cursory requirement before jumping on top of me and making passionate love. I'd never had sex with a woman who had so many tattoos, I thought.

And then the guilt flashed through my mind again. *Goddamn Catholic school upbringing — and Kate's all-knowing eye. Yes, she would know. I don't know how, but she had an uncanny sixth sense.*

I redirected my attention away from Natasha's face and down to the details of her art. It was an impressive mess, to say the least. The colors were diverse, but thematically tied a blend of yellow, red, and black, and anything that combination could produce. The paint evoked strong, abstract images of fire. The flames were fragments of faded, torn and half-burnt pages of old text. At the center was an artificially aged black and white print of Natasha, totally naked, sitting cross-legged on an old bean bag. In the nude photo, her tattoos were not excessive. They perfectly fit her body, which was in great shape yet voluptuous. She looked even better naked than I'd imagined — at least in that carefully posed piece of art.

"So what do ya' think?

"It's amazing," I said.

"Seriously?" She said.

"Yes, seriously. Your photo looks great too."

Of course, I was *only* referring to the nude photo in the middle of the piece. And I realized how unfair it was. She was vulnerable — on display. Her art and her body were exposed, hoping, begging for approval. All I had to do was make a few positive comments about the piece — how they fit, how the lines were well-crafted, how the tone was professional. Maybe offer a question or soft criticism so the compliments would sound more credible. It would all be bullshit anyway, I thought. I only cared about her naked photograph in the middle. I couldn't stop staring at her crossed legs and full breasts. It reminded me of the old Playboys I used to steal from my dad. And I couldn't help but visualize Natasha stepping slowly in front of the canvas without a stitch of clothing on and proceeding to seduce me.

Natasha rested the right side of the canvas against the bookcase and revealed what she had been hiding. She wasn't completely naked, but almost. She had on plain black underwear and a bra—that was it. She giggled a bit in feigned embarrassment, but she knew she had a good body. She *had* to.

"You know, there's another reason I wanted you to come over…"

Yeah, that was becoming pretty clear: casual sex.

"I need more black and white photos of me for the next piece I make," she explained. "And I need someone to take pictures so I can start on it today, while I'm inspired."

Yeah, I thought, and I just looked like a decent photographer from the way I was staring at that ancient door in the restaurant, and the way I gawked at you during lunch? I had a big scruffy beard, so of course I was thoughtful and artistic and uniquely opinionated. Either that or a big creep. Honestly, I didn't really care what kind of misconceptions she had about me.

I felt lucky—*and cursed.*

She was desperate for approval and I was desperate for other reasons. Desperate because my life had been falling apart and this ridiculous day was somehow smashing it all in my face. I closed my eyes for a second in disbelief as a stream of flashes flooded through me:

Natasha's naked body on top of me.

The sensation of her tattooed, unfamiliar skin.

But she was not Kate.

Guilt.

Natasha moaning. The new smell of her hair falling on my face.

More guilt.

Kate's reaction when she found out.

More guilt.

Yes, she would find out.

But did it even matter anymore?

Irrational fear.

I spotted another tattoo on the small of Natasha's back.

Fear.

— A fear of sexually transmitted diseases that was driven into me at a young age by a slew of Catholic nuns and priests. And the increased likelihood of dangerous promiscuity among aggressive, attractive, heavily tattooed women.

Natasha turned and slowly squatted down to grab her camera case on the floor.

Jesus Christ!

More guilt – from Kate's sad face crying the last time I –

"I have to go." I said.

"What!?" Natasha protested in disbelief. "Are you serious?"

"I'm sorry." I said. "I feel bad and I don't really know why, and I don't know you and…" I stalled, not sure if I wanted to say it, or if I had any reason to say it, "…and I have a girlfriend."

The look of disappointment on her face was unmistakable, as if I had promised her a million dollar commission for her artwork, and then rescinded. Or maybe her look of disgust was simply that I had assumed too much about this free-spirited artist who maybe had nothing more than a distaste for excessive clothing.

"Are you sure you have a girlfriend?" she asked, implying that I could wish Kate away.

I hesitated. In retrospect, it was a great question. I was tempted, of course, and she knew it. Women are much better at reading people. I've come to accept that as a scientific fact.

"Yes, I am," I said. It was a complete lie.

I said "Sorry" again as I turned and walked toward the door.

"Well, too bad for you," Natasha said.

Yeah, too bad I had a conscience. Too bad I still felt committed and conscious of Kate's trust and feelings for some stupid reason. Too bad I went to Catholic school for twelve years. Too bad I wasn't younger, artistic, impulsive, and willing to take risks and live in the present moment. Too bad I was older,

*boring, stuck, scared, guilt-ridden, and too comfortable in my
sunny hometown to actually do anything different with my life.*

Ghetto is Not an Adjective

I had no clue what time it was as I walked away from Natasha's toward the closest bus stop on 30th street. *Ask the bus driver,* I thought. If I had just asked the bus driver earlier that day, two detours could've been avoided. Thankfully, the bus arrived at almost the same time I made it to the bus stop bench—just long enough to notice the cheesy image of a slick, dark-haired real estate agent dominating the personal ad on the backrest.

I stepped on the bus and flashed my all-day pass as if I were a public transit veteran. At the risk of blowing my cover, I asked the heavy set driver if I was on the right bus—the one that continued through South Park, Golden Hill and headed into downtown. He confirmed this with surprisingly little annoyance in his voice. I thought about asking him more questions. I had already assumed and erred too much that day. So I lingered by the driver, though there were a few people behind me, waiting to get on. I felt a pressure that told me I could only ask one more question.

"What time is it?" I asked him.

His head didn't move. His eyes were laser focused straight ahead. I thought he didn't hear me at first.

"3:26," he said curtly. "My *job* is to drive," he added. "Next question's gonna' cost you a dollar."

Jesus Christ, where had the time gone!? — I'd felt the same way at my last birthday party. How had all that time passed and yet I'd accomplished so little?

I picked a seat toward the rear, closer to the Mexican junior high students in the back than the disabled people in the front. Sitting in the back seemed more interesting because the students were actually talking to each other, lounging along the rear wall and on the side benches, making it a communal area — everyone facing each other. I didn't fit in, but I wasn't trying to either. I was just there to eavesdrop on the way to downtown.

The most vocal were two teenaged Latina girls with tightly pulled back black hair and heavy eyeliner. They were sitting adjacent to me, chatting away, occasionally going into a whiny, sing-songy Spanglish that was harsh on the ears. A Mexican male with dark-rimmed glasses sat across from them. He looked more like a young college student who had recently adopted Che Guevara as his personal hero — or at least his fashion consultant. We both sat there listening to the girls' chatter, without staring directly at them, and knowingly glanced at each other once — aware that we were distracted by the same thing.

As the bus started toward downtown, the two teeny-boppers' piercing voices, foul language, and shrieking laughter was becoming intolerable. They were in that junior high stage when obnoxiousness and vulgarity made one more popular amongst their insecure peers. I guess it was pretty normal teenage banter. Then they said it — a word I had previously given little to no consideration.

"That's so ghetto!" the skinnier one said.

"*You're* ghetto," the other snapped back.

The Che Guevara guy's eyes lit up and filled with fire. His brow lowered in distress. He carefully observed the girls now.

I didn't get it, but he had obviously reacted to the word "Ghetto." I'd heard "ghetto" used in such a way before, but thought nothing of it aside from its technical misuse.

"I am *not* ghetto," the skinny one replied sassily.

"You are tooo GHETTO!" the other repeated.

"What?" Che interrupted them.

He seemed unduly agitated, but more out of intense philosophical interest than raw aggression—as if he were an impassioned, self-proclaimed professor of social justice. Maybe it was the thick-rimmed eyeglasses. Whatever it was, the girls stopped their bickering. Shocked, they turned their noses and blackened eyebrows up at him.

"What does that mean?" he asked them.

"What are you talkin' about?" the skinny one said, defensively.

They weren't ready for interruption or disapproval from a stranger on the bus. They were unaware of the gravity. So was I.

"What does calling someone "Ghetto" mean?" Che clarified.

The two girls looked both surprised by the question and puzzled by what may have seemed like too obvious of an answer—an answer to a question they'd probably never considered. The more talkative one with flashy fingernails and a black Sharpie in her hand spoke up.

"'Ghetto' means—," she hesitated, "Bad—you know—dirty or poor or ugly looking."

"—All those things," her friend chimed in with a thicker accent.

Che nodded and smirked in both acknowledgement and disappointment, as though he expected that exact answer from them. Then he leaned over more deliberately, crouching toward them with his elbow on his knees. He pushed his glasses higher up on his nose. It looked as if he were preparing to spring on them.

"Ghetto is not an adjective," he said in a calm yet commanding voice.

The two girls turned to each other in what seemed to be confusion and discomfort. By the looks on their faces, they probably didn't even know what an 'adjective' was.

Che repeated, with growing intensity and clear enunciation: "*Ghetto* is not an adjective. It is a noun. It's the place where I live."

All of a sudden, that the bus was moving South, that there were over twenty other people on it, and that it was the middle of a comfortable San Diego afternoon didn't matter. This large vehicle had become a vessel—a stage—for a poetic, passionate soul to express to two captive girls (and the other passengers) his perspective on what "ghetto" meant to him. They had no idea that their use of "ghetto" might disturb someone so deeply. And neither did I. But it must have meant the world to Che because he rose to the occasion. He continued what first appeared to be part soapbox rant and part spoken-word poetry:

"For me it's Barrio Logan to be exact, but that lone fact is insignificant."

He made the words *exact* and *fact* punch us in the face with emphasis, rhythm, and a cadence that sounded well-practiced. He continued, to the girls' surprise, with a driving sense of purpose:

"There's no Sherman, or Logan, or Shelltown to those on the outside looking in.

It's all 'ghetto' to them.

Safely kept at a distance--

mostly imagined on pixelated screens

or glanced through car windows at high speeds.

And it's okay, as long as we stay in it,

except in transit

between working kitchens and keeping things clean..."

Che paused and took a big breath for the first time. He glanced at me, noticed that I was paying attention, then glared back at the now more attentive girls—in awe by what one word had sparked in this guy.

"*Ghetto* is not an adjective because it's a place

that does not fit one description

like crime-ridden, gang-infested, dirty manifestation

no doubt a result of our news and TVs

bombarding us with well-edited crime scenes.

Yes, I've seen a young teen

with a shiny silver gun in his hand

To Be Frank Diego

and tats in between

sirens and gunshots,

yelling and screams

boxed in by conveniently constructed freeways

that still segregate

pollution and stress causing our health to disintegrate.

Immobilized by poor public education

Disconnected teachers waiting for vacations

— and their credentials

Leaving untapped potential to linger in subservience

Like servants, we're kicked around all day

Picking, cooking, and cleaning — praying for change.

But how will this change?

When words like *ghetto* are washed into our brains

Everyday, by TVs, movies, and video games

And you!

When I hear you utter the word *ghetto* in disdain

It pains me to associate my house and my name

It's this invisible virus that infects us the most

Through a simplistic, linguistic bacterial host

A flippant adjective for some — a reality for most.

Madness has turned the word *ghetto* into an adjective.

Unfortunately, for now, it's where I live."

    Che took another deep breath. He had the attention of every passenger. He had to have practiced his poem at least a hundred times. The delivery was polished and near perfect. Everyone on the bus had listened, and were either waiting for the next line, or for some authority figure to intervene and pull the plug on this social rebel. I was impressed by Che's courage, presence and passion—but he wasn't finished. Sensing his audience had grown, Che amplified his volume when he resumed:

"However, I see *ghettos* that don't fit your ugly descriptions...

I see families at dinner in joint celebrations

I see kids playing soccer and scores of elation

I see the faces of the elderly in exaggeration

I see friends greeting and laughing at the bus stop

Even a rare scene with a considerate cop.

I see houses painted vibrant colors

that suburban HOA's would ban

I hear loud music, passion and see all-natural tans

I feel the pulse of the moment and the beating of drums

Beautiful murals, loving people, and harmless bums

So, if not the mainstream media and not the TV

At least let's start it—just you and me

To Be Frank Diego

And not ghettoize our lives

 our roots and our ways

Know the meaning of our words and question and say:

'Yes, I live in one of many ghettos

— often separated, misrepresented, or ignored.

I'm in a favela. I'm in a slum.

 But I don't need any more slumlords!

So don't trap us with your words

that berate the place I live

And remember, please remember:

Ghe-tto

  Ghe-tto

   Ghe-tto

 Is NOT an adjective..."

Everyone was silent as the bus rolled to its next stop. I had never seen such an impromptu performance, and I doubt anyone else on that bus had either. We all should have applauded in unison. We should've given him an award, but we didn't. It all happened too fast.

When he finished, Che hastily grabbed his messenger bag and stood up as the bus doors opened. For some unknown reason, he glanced at me and tossed a folded paper on my lap. It was his poem. Before I could look up and say thanks, he was gone. A few people praised him as he passed by their seats, but he exited without another word, adding even more dramatic effect to the whole scene.

I looked out the window and watched him walk triumphantly southbound down the hill toward Barrio Logan—the 'ghetto' he was referring to. I had never been there—never thought of going there, actually. It was south of the 94 freeway and I seldom went there out of habit and lack of necessity, I guessed. It made me question my own Mexican-ness though. Barrio Logan was the "most Mexican" neighborhood in San Diego, yet I'd never set foot in it. And Che was right. I had no idea what it was like in that, or any other so-called ghetto—only what others had made me believe over the years. His recitation was unbelievable, and his last line lingered in my head:

'Ghetto is NOT an adjective!'

I looked back to my left at the two teenage girls. They were both scrunching their faces together in confusion and disapproval—almost disgust. They whispered a few inaudible words back and forth until the skinnier one blurted out:

"El esta *loco!*"

It seemed that the intended audience for Che's epic poem had already dismissed him as crazy. They didn't get it, which was a shame. Then they resumed their gossiping.

'Go Chargers', I thought.

And then I noticed a bumper sticker on one of the Mexican girl's otherwise photo-littered binder cover.

It read: *Go Chargers!*

I'm not joking.

Downtown

I was finally going west again, and the bus had made it far enough south to be out of the refitted upper-middle class zone and into the Barrio. The streets were no longer tree-lined with cute, vintage boutiques. Now we cruised by mostly chain link fences and graffiti-streaked walls that protected weed-ridden and plantless front yards. More people walked on the sidewalks and waited at bus stops. And the skin color of most pedestrians was noticeably darker than those only a mile to the north. My Southern California hometown was beginning to look much less 'fine' than advertised.

Our bus was soon descending the westward facing slope of Golden Hill, overlooking downtown. The skyline, with the Pacific coast in the background, was refreshing to see. But it wasn't the skyline of a full-grown city. It seemed more of a carefully developed imitation of one. As we rolled closer, I was reminded that during the day the downtown sidewalks were rarely crowded. They were not bustling with fast-paced business people, workers and shoppers of all stripes like a New York or San Francisco. It was only at night that 5th avenue restaurants, bars, and stores came alive, and the street grew a lively, albeit cosmetic pulse.

The bus bounced and leveled out as we entered the smallish urban grid. I was reminded, again, that being downtown was not part of my original plan—a plan that had become laughable. And I wondered what might happen to my larger plans if I simply just let things naturally unfold more often and didn't plan at all—or let myself fall into the plans of others.

Kate. Had she tried to call me? Would she show up in PB? Would I even make it in time?

Along with nearly everyone else, I stepped off the bus at the Park Blvd Transit Center. I guess it was considered a transit 'center' because of the one trolley line and two bus stops there—each one on opposite sides of the block. Like a pack animal, I followed the large crowd moving toward the nearby beeping trolley. I jumped onboard without thinking. It wasn't till I was squeezed in tightly that I realized I wasn't sure which way it was heading—north or south. I needed it to go north.

I tried to ask the man standing next to me which way we were going, but he didn't speak English. So I asked the woman sitting closest to me. She didn't speak English either. I was sorely reminded that though my father could speak Spanish fluently and I had taken over four years of Spanish in school, I didn't know how to ask the simple question: "Which direction does this go?" Even if I could piece the right words together, I'd be too embarrassed to say them out loud with my Americano accent.

'May I just call you Frank?' a voice echoed in my head.

The doors closed and we started moving south toward Mexico. *Did I really make another stupid mistake this late in the game? Had Miss Saigon thrown a rare Vietnamese curse on me? Or was this all happening in a particular sequence that was somehow meant to be? —No, that was some dumb thing a new-agey ex-girlfriend said to me a long time ago.*

Either way, I realized it wasn't a catastrophic mistake. Though the route map above the interior window did show Tijuana-Border as its final destination, the next stop would be no more than a few blocks away — or six.

And they were a surprisingly long six blocks. I guess anytime you're heading in the opposite direction — and are conscious of doing so — the time in transit seems longer and more aggravating.

The trolley glided through what is now called East Village. It was a brand new section of downtown designated as the city's squeaky-clean version of Soho, with buildings so freshly constructed, spotless and colorless, it looked more like an architect's model than a lived-in reality.

I jumped out as soon as the doors sprang open at the new Petco Park stop, as if my sudden sense of urgency and waiting in the proper place would make the northbound line arrive any faster. Though I shouldn't have, I felt confident that I didn't need to ask about what line to take back. There were only two directions I could go: north or south.

I crossed the tracks and put one foot up on a cement planter to stretch my leg. My hamstrings and feet were already sore. In mid stretch I realized that I was trying to do yoga moves inconspicuously and half-heartedly, in effect taking any sense of the yoga benefit out of them. Finishing my toe-touch, I looked beyond my own shoe and admired the economic heart of the new downtown: Petco Park baseball stadium.

I felt torn. One part of me wanted to rant about how the poor and homeless had been forcefully removed to make room for the new stadium and surrounding condos. How it was all about property values, big investors, and new, chic commercial space; and how the Spanish colonial padres and the Padres' baseball executives were essentially in the same business: exploiting and profiting off of the natives.

The other part of me didn't care, and wondered when the baseball season started, and thought about what kind of beer I'd be drinking as I watched a game with my friends — or girlfriend (if I had one). I imagined the warm weather and the agreeable conversation interrupted only here and there with fans yelling this:

'Go Padres!'

But I wondered if I could do that anymore, because I had to admit: That's what I had spent the majority of my life *doing* in San Diego.

Stingaree

When the northbound trolley arrived, I waited as the largest number of black and brown people I'd ever seen in San Diego poured out through its doors. I imagined many of them worked nights in the kitchens and messy underbellies of the chi-chi clubs and restaurants downtown. I imagined they would slave away till dawn, caught in a schedule that left them little time to see their own children. And on occasion, when the economy dragged, I pictured them being scapegoated for taking jobs away from 'decent' Americans.

I boarded the trolley and watched it fill up as rush hour approached. Soon our cartoonish, advertisement-covered car began to move northbound. The revamped area reminded me of the one new East Village place I had actually been to: *Stingaree* — which reminded me of when I brought Kate there.

Stingaree is an upscale club — or at least it tried to be. Most patrons had to dress well and wait in long lines and pay $30-50 to get in. Then they had to pay another $100 if they wanted to sit down and attempt to have a conversation beneath the booming dance music. I didn't like the place very much. I thought entering and sitting down should be free. I also thought water should be free. However, I did like one thing about *Stingaree*. It had an interesting hint of local history.

The time Kate and I went there, about a year ago, we didn't have to wait in line or pay to get in. We were escorted inside by an alluring young woman named Lara who was a manager there. By coincidence, we'd bumped into her at the door. Lara used to be one of those rare distracting college students who sat in the back of my history class. That night, in her short, black cocktail dress, Lara looked like she should have and could have been in Playboy magazine.

Once we passed through security, Lara grabbed my hand to lead me — us — through the packed crowd. Some of the carousers were idly standing, others dancing to the thunderous house music. But there seemed to be no designated dance area. It all blended together in a sea of humans searching for the epicenter of the party, looking for photo opportunities to later impress their Facebook friends.

Kate grabbed my other hand and trailed behind me through the crowd. I almost forgot she was back there for a minute because I was preoccupied by the guiding hand of Lara — her black strapless dress shifting just below her tan shoulder blades, as she confidently cut through a sea of young clubbers.

Lara led us to the second floor bar, kindly ordered us free drinks, and thanked me for coming in. When she hugged me goodbye I got a whiff of her intoxicating, unfamiliar perfume. *Unfamiliar was intriguing. She was intriguing.* Then Lara went back to work, disappearing into the crowd.

Kate grabbed my hand, but when I looked back at her she didn't say a word. I leaned close to her ear and asked if she wanted to go upstairs to the rooftop because the music was so loud inside. She shrugged her shoulders and stared at the people passing by. So I led her to the open-air third floor where it wasn't so hard to move around and find a place to sit. The look on Kate's face showed an uncommon hint of insecurity, I guessed, because of all the Lara-types inside the place (and Lara herself).

I found a cushiony lounge chair to sit down in and leaned back. That's when a security guard appeared out of nowhere and said to me with exaggerated authority:

"This area is VIP only."

"How do you know I'm not a VIP?" I asked.

"Did you reserve a table and buy a bottle?" he said.

"Nope." I said.

"Then you're not a VIP," he informed me.

"How much is a bottle?"

"They start at a hundred dollars," he said.

I looked at him with a bit of surprise, but it didn't really shock me. I'd heard about this ridiculous sort of thing. And I supposed the exorbitant prices were for two types: the newly rich, and those who wanted to pretend they were rich, if only for one night. I didn't fit into either type.

The rest of that night at *Stingaree* was spent with Kate on the rooftop, standing on tired feet and drinking pricey cocktails. She talked about politics and gossip at her school — mostly about colleagues and their slacker tendencies. She called it "debriefing," and it began to feel much like any other night in our apartment — except that we had to pay if we wanted sit down, and bass-heavy music filled in the gaps of our predictable conversation.

So I changed the subject. I told Kate that the new *Stingaree* nightclub sat in the center of what was the old Stingaree red light district — the slimiest, sleaziest, and

99

roughest part of downtown. If one was transported to the 1930's Stingaree, I explained, they would be witness to a number of prostitutes, drug-dealers, drunkards, and other criminal elements. Not too much different than the contemporary version, I suppose, but there was a big difference back then: Japanese people.

I told Kate that the Stingaree was once the Japanese section of San Diego because most of the white communities wouldn't let Japanese people live in their neighborhoods. In the notorious Stingaree, Japanese-Americans built a community and stayed in it, or close to it, for fear of being beaten by white vigilante groups who justified hate crimes as the defense of American freedom.

From what I read, the Japanese were doing all right in the Stingaree district, starting businesses and networks and such—building families and a sense of community. Then, in 1942, the U.S. government came into the Stingaree, rounded up all the Japanese people, forced them to leave their property and most possessions, loaded them on buses, and shipped them to deserts in the middle of nowhere.

"That's where the Japanese were imprisoned for the next three years," I said.

"Why?" Kate asked.

I explained that some important Americans—in politics and the media—sparked an anti-Japanese propaganda campaign after the attack on Pearl Harbor. The were afraid that Japanese people who had been living in (even born in) the United States would sabotage America from within. So they rounded up over two hundred thousand people and put them in prison.

"Was there any evidence against them?" Kate asked.

Evidence? I told Kate that The United States apparently didn't need any evidence when fear, a generalized sense of revenge, and paranoia would suffice. That and racism, I added.

"Racism?" she asked.

I explained that there was no equivalent government policy that demanded a mass round up of our other World War II enemies — German and Italian-Americans — in domestic prison camps. There were no ads or posters or radio shows calling German and Italian-Americans evil, vicious, vermin.

Kate didn't seem to care for my story much. She focused on her drink. She was probably more concerned about our waning relationship and the truth about *us*. And, in hindsight, I was probably trying to avoid that very subject by telling old stories that had nothing to do with us.

The end of that night on the rooftop at *Stingaree* was telling. Kate stared at the skyline as she finished her drink. I looked down at the area where I imagined the Japanese internment began.

"Unbelievable," she said. About what I wasn't sure.

I remember taking that last moment to look around the rooftop lounge again to see if I could spot — not another remnant of local history — a different kind of distraction: Lara.

El Cabron

The memory of that night out with Kate had removed me from my crowded trolley reality. What brought me back was a Mexican guy in his mid-fifties with a red baseball cap sitting across from me.

"Hola. Como estas?" the Mexican guy said when he caught my glance.

"Bien," I replied.

It came out easier and more naturally than I expected, but then I added, "Y tu, como estas?" And, while four futile years of Spanish classes told me that phrase was correct, it sounded as if I was a bad TV actor trying to force an authentic Mexican accent.

"Bien, bien. Gracias," the man responded, but then he fired off a few Spanish sentences in a row, and I was instantly lost. I nodded to pretend I understood, but I knew the next thing I'd say to him would have to be in English.

That's when a scruffy, white homeless-looking guy, who I hadn't noticed was sitting next to me, interrupted:

"Where you from?" he asked me, as if it was an appropriate greeting.

His facial hair hadn't been shaved for a few days and his eyes bulged behind his lightly amber-tinted glasses.

"I'm from here," I said.

He looked surprised when I responded in English. I think he assumed I spoke Spanish better than English, which, if true, made me feel more Mexican than I did seconds before when the Mexican guy said hello to me in Spanish.

"Didya' go to college?" he asked.

I wasn't sure where he was going with his line of questioning. I wasn't sure if he was sober or sane. "I did," I said.

"Whudya' study?" he asked.

"History." I answered, then looked across at the Mexican guy who looked confused by the English. I was confused too—about the direction of our conversation. Because proximity made them hard to avoid, I turned to the white guy and began to ask him, "Wha—

"—History: Good!" he interrupted. "Then you know that Latin is not a language! And if Latin is not a language, and it never existed, then Latino doesn't mean nothin'! So why're all these people runnin' around callin' themselves *Latinos*?"

Latin? Latinos? Where was he getting this stuff? With a goofy emphasis on *Latinos* he ogled me, then did the same to the Mexican guy. Before I had a chance to respond — *Did I even want to respond to this whackjob?* — the Mexican guy jumped in at him with his heavy accent:

"Jew are crazy!" Then he turned to me, "El esta loco!" — as if I didn't understand his English version.

"Hey there you son-of-a-bitch," the white guy said to him, "Just because the Nazis didn't—

"Callate, Cabron." The Mexican guy snapped, "Jew haf mental problems. Dios mio!"

"Speaking of Jews," the white guy said, looking to me, "They're like Latinos cuz they never had a real name neither. It was all made up because Hitler…" Pausing, he pointed his finger in the Mexican guy's face: "And you're trying to sell me whiskey for a goddamn dollar a pop!?"

I was lost.

"Jew are crazy, Cabron!" the Mexican guy shouted.

They both sounded crazy. And it became apparent that these two had previously met each other's acquaintance, and that they likely had the same nonsensical argument on a regular basis.

The white guy threw out a few more disconnected historical references. *Jesus, could that be me someday*? Thankfully, they both stood up when the trolley came to the next stop, and continued their bickering as they exited and parted ways on the sidewalk.

With the trolley gliding toward the late afternoon sun, I felt I was finally making progress, and was still confident about getting to my car in time.

The Runner

Looking out the trolley window, I couldn't help but notice a flash on the sidewalk, right along side me. A slender guy wearing a white T-shirt and raggedy blue jeans was running barefoot at full speed, almost at pace with the trolley. His pumping arms carried sandals in one hand and what looked like a black notebook in the other. His longish brown hair was blown back by the wind. When he blew past three guys in suits, I wondered how his dirty bare feet were holding up on the hard cement. More than that, I wondered why the hell he was running. *Was he a thief? On a bad acid trip? Or was he trying to catch the trolley at the next stop?*

The next stop was Santa Fe Station — the Spanish mission revival train stop built especially for the Balboa Park Exposition in 1915. The ceramic tiled roof, off-white walls, and wide arches suggested that it was made by Spaniards in the 18th century. A tourist might imagine the wood beams shipped in from Granada. This wasn't the case though. The truth was that it was less than a hundred years old, and built for visitors bound for pretty Balboa Park with its matching style and architecture.

But I was more interested in the barefoot runner, who had caught up to the trolley as it slowed to a halt. Dozens of people exited and entered, and the panting runner just happened to come and sit next to me, propping one filthy foot on the adjacent bench.

We didn't exchange a single word though. I acknowledged his existence with brief eye contact and a nod, and he did the same before looking to the opposite window. Then the runner opened his well-worn journal and held the pen in his left hand, ready to write. I couldn't help but glance at the lined notebook paper and peep at what he was about to jot down.

He wrote: *"Downtown San Diego. Third time I've run down a train..."*

And he paused after the dot, dot, dot. I imagined he was reflecting on other train chasings, and it turned out he was. His journal was almost flat on his lap, easy to read from where I sat, so I felt okay about snooping. From my angle, I guessed he wouldn't be able to sense me stealing glances at his writing.

He flipped through the stained pages, which were covered with writing in all kinds of colors. He stopped on a page near the beginning. I read his entry:

Chased a train today in Padova, Italy to get to Genova to sail to Caribbean... Sailboat there is smaller than I thought... captain oddly focused on my American passport, but I got the job!

The page was dated "June." Maybe the entry was from six, or even eighteen months ago. Beneath it was a rough, but decent sketch of a sailboat — probably the one he'd sailed on from Genova.

The runner's head quickly moved up from his journal, so I looked away. I was almost sure he didn't notice me. But if he had noticed, he didn't seem to care much because he returned to his notebook seconds later and turned two pages:

Just escaped from Barbados by ferry. Had to swim away from boat while docked in private bay. The captain and crew got sketchy when drunk. Talked about taking my passport that night...Think they were talking in code about drugs and guns,

*then passed out drunk… Thank god I got out of that one.
Crazy…*

It was a little too crazy — almost unbelievable. He must
have ziplock bagged his belongings before swimming
away that night. He must have inched his way into the
water to avoid making noise while the crew slept. There
must have been sharks in that water, and then the
Barbadians who eyed this suspicious foreigner as he
walked through their town in drenched clothes.

I took a closer look at the journal. It looked like it had
been through hell — creased in many places, faded, and
water damaged. It looked like an artifact. The way this
guy held it, I could tell the journal had become one of his
prized possessions. I caught him smiling to himself and
shaking his head. I guessed he was thinking about that
extraordinary episode. Then he closed the journal on his
lap.

The view from the moving trolley was much less
interesting than the runner's notebook. Facing west, the
tops of skinny palm trees spotted the horizon, along with
large Navy ships docked in the bay. That view soon gave
way to barbed wire coiled on chain link fences that
protected the fleets of rental cars waiting in parking lots
surrounding the airport. And the only thing buzzing by
my window were close ups of green, drought resistant
vines purposefully grown to cover a plain concrete wall.
Until we slowed to a stop.

The only reason I vividly remember that stop — the
reason why it matters at all — is because it brought Miss
Saigon's wrinkled face back to the front of my mind, and
completely vindicated her with one chance sighting. Our
trolley was stopped at an intersection where a #6 bus was
idling. *The #6 was the bus I had been on with Miss Saigon
earlier, the one that broke down; the one she kept telling me*

would take me to the — And that's when my eyes caught the large green street sign with white lettering. The name of that street: *BEECH.*

Son of a bitch! She had been telling me the truth all along — kind of. I shook my head in disbelief.

Then I heard the pages of the runner's journal open again. I casually faked interest in the view to my left and peered down at his open diary. He'd flipped back to one of the first entries:

Just chased a train in Tangier, Morocco to get Matt. Didn't catch it. I'll wait for three days to hear from him, then leave Morocco. Nothing more I can do.

I didn't see a date, but it had to be before Italy, unless there was no chronological order to his writing. *Was this guy for real?* He looked no older than thirty and he'd been tramping around the world, chasing trains, and in full-blown adventure mode. And now he was in San Diego of all places. *Why San Diego?* It seemed boring in comparison.

…Matt emailed from Marrakesh today. Thinks he was drugged. Doesn't remember much. No details. Woke up in Fez! …Seems rattled but okay now. Told me he's flying back to NYC. Feeling sorry for him. His trip was cut short. I doubt he'll travel like this again.

The runner put his hand over the page and looked up from his notebook. My eyes went straight to the window again, as if the chain link fences and palm trees were too fascinating to miss. *Did he know I was reading his journal? Or was he pondering the regret he had about his inability to help his friend back in Morocco?*

Again, if he had sensed that I was reading over his shoulder, then he didn't seem to mind. He moved his hand, flipped back to the pen-marked page and continued writing:

Downtown San Diego. The third time I've run down a train... Got the wired money, finally. Grabbing last minute supplies tonight and back to the boat. Sailing out early tomorrow for Mexico.

He placed the pen inside the journal, closed and banded it shut. *Where was he sailing to in Mexico? What was next? How did he live like this? Who just wired him money? Was it his parents, an employer, or some shady illegal arrangement? — It wasn't out of the realm of possibility.* He seemed like a decent globetrotting guy, but who knew. He could have been anything from a writer for an adventure travel magazine, to a fugitive running from the law, or part of an international crime ring.

And what had started his journey? Had he jumped on the first departing cargo ship from his homeport without a penny to his name, or was he a college-educated trust fund baby searching for anything exotic and exciting?

The problem was that I couldn't ask him any of these questions because I had already read too much. Because I couldn't ask, nor forcefully grab his journal and read more, I settled for imagining his next move in a vicarious, first person entry that flashed across the screen in my cinematic mind's eye:

Put the $10,000 in cash in the boat safe. Double check the supplies. Hug the Mexican coastline going south for a week. Dock in La Paz for a break. Submit my next story from Zihuatanejo.

Yes, I imagined the runner as a traveling writer. It made sense to me—a gentler Hunter S. Thompson type who injected himself into the story, and into dicey situations. He traveled around the world submitting first hand stories that were so rich and twisted they were hard to believe. Occasionally his publisher would wire him money from major cities on his voyage. Maybe he was working on a novel too.

And maybe I imagined him this way because it's what I really wanted to do. I wanted to travel off the beaten path. I wanted more time to be creative and write. But it seemed there were always excuses and rationalizations, or commitments keeping me from these yearnings. The runner made me think of my limited, consuming San Diego life and all the places I hadn't been— all the trains I hadn't chased.

And maybe even the ones I'd jumped on, but were going in the wrong direction.

I thought of Kate.

I thought of my strange day off, and how many more "days off" my job would give me.

The trolley arrived at the Old Town stop. The doors hissed as they opened, and the runner was on his way, ahead of everyone else.

The runner and I had not exchanged a word, but sometime in the future, if he ever came across this story, maybe he would recognize himself. And if he did, I'd want to say at least one thing to him:

Thanks for the inspiration.

Raul

It was the end of the line so everyone got off, most in a rush to connect to the idling eastbound train. The Old Town stop was the closest to Pacific Beach the trolley system could take me. From there I had to figure out which bus would bring me the rest of the way. I should've been there hours before, but I could only blame myself and my inexperience (and no longer Miss 'Beech Street' Saigon) for my detour.

I followed the exiting crowd as I watched the eastbound trolley coast down the rails. I could see that buses were waiting on both sides of the tracks. The spot was a major hub for transfers, with foot traffic of all shapes and sizes bustling around more than any other non-urban place I'd been to that day. Trolleys were coming and going; buses arriving and departing. And everyone seemed to know where to go except me.

I noticed more buses on the other side so I walked down the stairs, through the underpass, and toward the bus stops. I scanned the area for a schedule and spotted a board labeled 'Information' that put a little hop back in my step. I squinted at the chart that was pressed and protected under a hard plastic panel.

I studied the schedule, miraculously beginning to comprehend some of it. I used my index finger to scan. When I got to the Pacific Beach bound bus, the numbers on that row were covered by a rogue piece of cardboard that had shifted inside the display board. *Of course – once I figured out how to read one of these things, the only information*

I needed was covered up! What bus would take me to Pacific Beach? That's all I needed to know.

"Jesus Christ," I said, not intending to be heard.

"Jew nid help?" asked a Mexican teenager with a thick but understandable accent.

He must have been standing close by and either heard me or noticed the discontented look on my face. I nodded at him, appreciative of his good sense of timing. He had one iPod headphone in his far ear, and squinted his right eye almost completely shut while he spoke to me, facing the setting sun.

"Yeah, thanks," I said.

"What bus jew nid?" he said, then smiled and corrected himself with a well enunciated: "Do-you-nid?"

He was polite and well-dressed for a teenager. He had on a preppy, blue dress shirt with the collar flared out a bit. His hair was gelled back.

"That's the problem," I said, "I don't know which bus goes to Pacific Beach."

"Oooh that's E-see. Get on noomber nine," he said.

"Number nine—that's it?" I asked.

"Jeah. E-see." He smiled—almost laughed—in amazement at my ignorance on the matter. Or maybe he was self-conscious about his heavy accent.

"It's right over there," he said. He pointed to the bus stop marked number nine.

"Thanks for the help." I said. He seemed like a nice kid.

"No pro-blem. My name is Raul."

He rolled the 'R' well and with ease.

"Thanks, Raul," I said. "My name's… Frank."

I thought about saying 'Francisco' with an attempt at a decent Mexican accent, but I didn't want to embarrass myself with a badly rolled *R* or a mispronounced vowel. I wished I knew how to speak Spanish. My dad once told me that I didn't want to learn Spanish when I was a little kid. He said I would run out of the room with my hands over my ears, making noises whenever he started speaking Spanish to me. So he stopped — gave up. I wished I hadn't done that. For the longest time I've always wanted to just understand and speak Spanish naturally — wake up one morning and start rambling with perfect fluency. Sometimes I dreamed about it. *Then* I would really be Mexican, I thought — or so I was meant to think.

"See jew later, mee-ster," Raul said, and gave me a smooth upward head nod before turning away.

At that instant, as the boy walked away, two men in plain black polo shirts and khakis emerged from nowhere to flank both sides of Raul. They said "U.S Border Patrol!" and grabbed his arms at the biceps. From about ten feet away, I stared, speechless as they rattled off a flurry of questions at him:

" — *Where are your papers?*

— *Where were you born?*

— *Where are your parents?*

— *Identification?*

— *Where do you live?*

113

– Your documents? Documentos!!!"

With each question, their voices grew more harsh and aggressive. *Could the boy even understand them?* Raul looked terrified. He looked as though he didn't know what to say. I watched his face transform from a kind, helpful kid to a scared, accused criminal in seconds. Before he could answer half their questions, before he could grasp the severity of the moment, they cuffed him and escorted him away, practically dragging him right by me. Raul glanced at me with a desperate, horror-stricken look on his face.

What could I do?

"Hey, what's going on here?" I said to the agents, as if I had any clout.

One agent shot a glare at me and said, "This guy's illegal. Mind your own business, buddy!" But he said it over his shoulder as they led Raul into the parking lot and out of my sight.

It angered me. I'd never witnessed a kid being arrested for no apparent reason. But I'd only witnessed the beginning—a brief scene. I had no idea what happened to Raul thereafter, or what the background story was. So as I sat there on the bench next to the number nine bus sign, I imagined the rest of it—Raul's story unfolding:

He was taken to an INS government van in the trolley station parking lot. He tried to ask the agents what was going on but they ignored him. Raul asked to call his mom, but instead of responding the agents pushed him up against the car and searched him. Then they put Raul in the back of a van with six other arrested adults and drove him to a processing center ten miles south, closer to the Mexican border. He sat in a waiting room and listened to immigration agents make derogatory jokes about Mexicans as if he couldn't understand English well enough to comprehend them. He also noticed posters of

Mexicans by border fences with target symbols superimposed on their backs and the title "This is the Enemy."

The agents told him that he couldn't call his mom or dad. That no one could help him anymore. That he had to sign papers and would be immediately 'relocated' to Tijuana, Mexico. He tried to hold his emotions together, thinking that if he was being treated as an adult then he should try to act like one. Raul refused to sign any papers out of confusion and a vague sense that he shouldn't sign anything without parental or legal advice.

With the same group of people he was driven, still cuffed, to a government building in San Ysidro, next to the border. His parents must have been worried sick about him because he usually made it home from school way before sunset. It was dark when the US immigration agents drove Raul across the border into Mexico, un-cuffed him, and returned his school backpack. By the time he was dropped off at the Tijuana orphanage that night, he cried. He couldn't believe he'd been deported on the way home from school, and found himself alone in one of the most dangerous cities in the world.

At least that's what I pictured happening. But I have to admit, that I may have imagined it all so clearly because I once heard a very similar story from another person named Raul: my dad.

Sea World

The screeching sound of the #9's brakes pulled me back
to the present. Once the tired looking passengers poured
out, I joined the line of people who quickly made the bus
almost full again. And after a brief period of waiting in my
blue plastic seat, we were off -- on what should have been
the last leg of my journey to PB.

The bus was soon approaching the beach and a major
city landmark: Sea World. I had only faint memories of
Sea World because I was a little kid the last time I'd been
there. I vaguely remembered a porpoise eating a smelly
dead fish out of my bare hand, and watching a killer
whale launch a human being twenty feet into the air with
its nose. I remember eating nachos and swinging on a
rope, and diving into a sea of red and blue ping pong
balls. That's about it. Since then it looked like Sea World
had added a rollercoaster and some other tall, pastel-
colored contraptions that were unrecognizable from the
road, and appeared to have no relation to sea life
whatsoever.

The end of my journey now seemed a foregone
conclusion. I would be in Pacific Beach in a matter of
minutes, I figured, giving me maybe an hour to spare.

As we slowed to a halt at the Sea World bus stop, I
noticed a large crowd of tourists on the sidewalk. I
assumed they were waiting for a charter bus or tour
company. But it soon became clear that the large group of
fluorescent hat, Bermuda short-wearing, sunburnt
Midwesterners were *all* trying to get on our bus. Subtle

sighs and gasps were released by my fellow passengers, who realized that the asses and elbows of representatives from almost every overweight state in the union would soon be crowding their personal space. One woman in the back even let out, "Ah, hell no," as the tour group bunched together outside the front door.

One of the first to board was a blonde, obese woman who had a knack for stating the obvious — and doing so loudly.

"Oh, this bus is gonna' fill up," she said as she turned back to watch her comrades file in. "Oh yeah," she said, to no one in particular, "We're getting real cozy in here."

I stood up, along with a few other passengers, to allow our fanny-pack-toting elders to sit down. A minute later everybody was packed in like sardines, which made that stationary rectangle-on-wheels warm up fast.

"Oooh, we have to get Betty in here," the same woman yelled to others in her group.

"Yeah, don't forget Betty," one of her friends said to the driver, as if he knew all bus passengers by name.

Betty was the middle-aged woman with badly dyed red hair, still waiting by the curb. She was the last one in what remained of the line at the bus's front door.

"Nope, we're full," the driver said to her as though it was a matter of national security: "Can't let anyone else on."

From the center of the bus I looked out at the sidewalk and noticed poor Betty standing at the door with a worried expression on her face.

"C'mon mister, can't you let in one more person," the yapper pleaded on Betty's behalf.

"No, we're full—and we have to move," the bus driver repeated.

Then the big blonde woman threw her body in the doorway and demanded: "Let her on. She's with us!"

The driver clarified, "You can get off, but she can't get on, Miss."

The woman turned to her friend Betty as if self-sacrifice were an unfamiliar concept; a word not in her vocabulary. Her pained wince revealed not empathy, but pity. Her expression made me think she felt sorry for Betty because, to her, there was no possible solution to this little dilemma.

Meanwhile, beads of sweat formed on the broad forehead of the man facing me. We were all uncomfortably packed in. Nobody moved. The bus idled. The driver and the large blonde lady had reached an impasse. The doors made a hiss and began to close.

I couldn't stand it anymore—but it wasn't about magnanimity. Sudden claustrophobia and the rank air had made me nauseous and brought on a slight headache. I decided I wouldn't stay on that bus. I pushed my way forward to the front doors saying "Excuse me, pardon me" along the way. As I passed between the bus driver and the gelatinous group leader I said to both of them, "I'll get off here."

The bus doors hissed and re-opened. Betty's so-called friend stopped chewing her gum and said, "That is sooooo nice of youuuu."

I suppose hindrances to progress had already become an expected feature of my day. I was getting used to them. And it wasn't really self-sacrifice. Real sacrifice was something I'd been fortunate enough to avoid most of my life.

I stepped down to Betty — sunburnt and short of breath on the sidewalk.

"You can get on now," I told her.

She looked confused. Rather than saying hello or thanking me, she asked in a thick Minnesotan accent:

"Who are youuu?"

I didn't respond with words. I just smiled politely at her and walked away. I didn't want to tell her I'd been trying to figure out the answer to that question since the 4th grade.

Kate Revisited

The fresh ocean air and the short distance remaining made my nausea and slight headache disappear. It also made the idea of finishing the home stretch on foot that much more appealing.

On the outskirts of PB, I figured the time it would take to walk to my car couldn't be more than forty minutes. And taking the bus all the way to the finish line at that point seemed a bit like cheating — like cutting corners — after becoming so accustomed to dealing with the challenge of unpredictable diversions. It didn't make much sense, I know. Maybe I was following my native Yaqui instincts. Maybe such things *did* happen for mysterious reasons that only my indigenous grandfather could've explained to me.

The bus sailed by, momentarily blocking my view of the setting sun and the coastal clouds that were rolling in. It was time to get my grey hooded sweatshirt out of my backpack. As usual, it was cooler near the beach. I headed northwest, hugging the vast parking lot of Sea World. From there the tall imported palms of Pacific Beach could be glimpsed in the distance.

Despite being on the verge of completing my almost failed plan; despite being surrounded by beautiful bays and oceans and parks and seagulls; despite being healthy and sort of young still, I felt a wave of sadness roll over me. My feet became heavier. As I dragged the soles of my shoes and felt distinct soreness in my left knee and foot, I started thinking about Kate again.

—*Her angry, crying face the last time I saw her. Her hope deflated.*

The last time I'd seen Kate was when she'd broken up with me—*or had I broken up with her?* I wasn't sure because I'd been actively avoiding the thought of that night ever since it happened.

I pictured Kate's face again—smiling this time. It seemed such a distant image. That's when my heart began to feel the weight of the truth and my throat tightened. My eyes watered as I thought about her.

And I couldn't conjure up another personal anecdote or historical aside because by then it had become all too obvious why I'd been doing this so often throughout the day. I remembered having once told my own students to seek the truth in history; to use the past to illuminate the present—not to avoid it.

The truth was that we'd broken up, and it had been four weeks since I last talked to Kate.

I clearly remembered that last talk of ours. It happened as the sunset and the amber rays dimly lit up our cozy, comfortable apartment. Actually, it felt more like Kate's apartment even though we split the rent evenly. Since we'd moved in she had decorated, furnished, rearranged, and controlled almost every aspect of the space. And that fateful evening—perhaps feeling tired of lacking control over our future together—she returned to a long-neglected subject after I'd finished cleaning off the kitchen counter.

"So, how are you feeling?" she asked me.

"Fine," I said. "I'm glad I don't have to plan much for tomorrow's class."

"No, I meant about us..." She hesitated, most likely fearing what that re-stated question might reveal. But she was probably too emotionally exhausted from waiting around for me to ask her to get married; tired of her girlfriends and her mother asking about what my "problem" was; tired of questioning my motives, my maturity and my character.

Though I didn't comprehend the big picture at the time, Kate was frustrated because things hadn't exactly happened according to her master plan. She was thirty-four years old, but wasn't married yet. She wasn't rich or financially set either. She didn't own a house or have a husband who owned a house. And she was feeling the pressure of age creeping up on her — her biological clock a daily reminder that her baby-making window was soon closing.

And there I was, looking at her with what likely appeared to be a dumb, numb expression on my face.

"I know we haven't talked about it in a while, but I need to know," Kate said.

What she meant by that was that we hadn't talked about marriage since the first time we'd talked about marriage, which took place six months prior to the night we *broke up*-broke up.

That conversation happened in bed, just before going to sleep. For the first time in two and a half years, she asked me what I thought about marriage. The 'with her' part was implied. I stalled a bit too long, and then told her that I didn't think about it very much; that I had no marriage plans. I admit that it came out abruptly and a bit harshly, but it was the truth. I had been drinking. And though I had once thought warmly about marrying Kate back in the beginning, I'd since grown uncharacteristically bored with the perfunctory recounting of our days. Tired of eating at fashionable restaurants I couldn't afford but she insisted on as necessary indulgence. Sick of going to sleep without having sex — or even the slightest inclination to do so — *way* before the age where that might be considered normal. It was a bleak vision of my future.

At any rate, my negative answer shocked her. Neither of us slept well that night and I felt the need to address it again, but our conversation the next day was relatively subdued for being so packed with emotion and doubt. I told her then that marriage could be a possibility, but that I wasn't ready or in any hurry to do so — with her or anyone. She explained to me that if I had no intentions of marrying her then I was just "wasting her time." It led to a mild separation for two weeks. However, a mix of lost love reactions — habit and comfort seeking, loneliness and hope — brought us back together on the unspoken condition that we would table the marriage subject. And we did. That is, until that evening six months later when she brought it up again and I still didn't have the answer she wanted:

"Let me be very clear: Do you plan on us getting married?" Kate asked me.

"Maybe?" I said.

"OK. I'll put it this way: Can you see us married in the not-too-distant future?" she asked.

"I honestly don't know." I said.

With that, Kate's face sunk below the straight expression she already wore. She sighed in abject disappointment. Her eyes glazed over. She was usually good at covering up her emotions. She was generally a kind, even-keeled person, but the look on her face turned to one of fierce disgust as our differences unraveled.

"Frank, I need a better answer than that. I —

"I'm just being honest, Kate. I'm sorry. It's hard to explain…" I said.

"What do you expect, an honesty award?" She raised her voice. "*Sorry*? That's all you've got is *sorry* after three years!"

I stood there biting down on the inside of my upper lip. It seemed like the only thing I could do in lieu of teleporting myself to a different planet. I didn't say a word. She went on:

"Look, I don't want to be pushy, but do you know the expression 'shit or get off the pot'?"

"I think I've heard that somewhere." I said.

"Well that's what I think this comes down to."

Our relationship had come down to a clichéd analogy about taking a crap? Had one of her friends or family members told her that that was my problem? That I had to —

"I need to know," Kate continued, "if you plan on marrying me, because if not then I need to make other plans. I need — I want to get married, and if you don't want to then…"

Her voice lost its breath and she began to cry. It made me want to cry too, until she added this a few seconds later, when she had regained her ability to speak:

"Yes or no? I need to know *now*."

I have to admit that it didn't exactly make me want to get down on one knee, offer a ring I didn't have (nor ever thought to buy), and commit to being with this woman for the rest of my life. It sounded demanding, desperate, and intransigent. *Was this what modern love had boiled down to?*

"Kate, all I can say right now is that I love you, but I don't know." I said.

I didn't add that she was putting quite a bit of pressure on me — and she wasn't taking the most romantic, or appealing approach. Kate looked me in the face, then her eyes drifted to an olive oil stain on the sleeve of my shirt. I'm not sure why I remember that detail, but I do. She gazed there for a few long, silent moments, then let out an injured, exasperated chuckle.

"I don't know what to say," she said.

Then she started crying again. It was as if I could see her heart sink and knew mine was soon to follow. My tears were welling up inside. I felt on the verge of crying again, anticipating an uncontrollable sob coming on as I moved forward to hug her in that painful moment.

"No," she said, "Please don't touch me."

Her frigid tone stopped my welling tears in their tracks. When I backed away I felt more distance between us than I imagined humanly possible for two people standing in the same room together. The conversation was over. It turned out that our big talk hadn't really been big, nor had much talking taken place. I figured it would have to be continued at a later date — perhaps in a few hours, or the following day.

"I'm going to go on a walk," I said. She nodded her bowed head without looking up at me. "I need to think about this alone and maybe…" I cut myself off when I realized I had nothing good to say. "I'll be back pretty soon."

I ended up walking around our North Park neighborhood for about two hours. During that time a prominent voice inside, call it instinct, was telling me that I couldn't marry Kate. That I wouldn't be happy, and that I couldn't make her happy, or help her achieve her ideal life — especially if I was suffering in a sea of boredom and regret all along the way. You don't marry someone because you *don't* want to ruin their plans and break their heart, I thought. You marry someone because spending the rest of your life with that person sounds like a great, beautiful idea — without any convincing or prodding.

Still, as I walked down endless blocks, half of me was concocting a plan to remedy Kate's sorrow. I thought of how to frame the idea of continuing together without self-imposing any pressure to get married. We could rethink the whole concept of the institution of marriage, I thought, so it could work for both of us. Something. Anything.

By the time I came back to the apartment, I was ready to talk it out like two mature adults. I was ready to compromise. I was ready to be open, yet speak my mind; be loving and sensitive, yet as truthful as I could be without doing any more damage. I opened the door and greeted Kate with a spark of renewed hope.

"Hi," I said.

She didn't respond. She was sitting on the couch, stoically reading a book.

"I was thinking…" I started.

"Um, I don't really care what you think." She said. "And there's really nothing more to talk about anyway."

" Well, I—"

" —And I don't want to hear whatever *bullshit* you have left to say to me," she said.

Kate had never pointed a cuss word so sharply at me before. She had never described any of my words as 'bullshit' either.

She added: "I don't think there's anything more to say, and I don't want you to sleep here tonight."

"What?" I said.

"I put most of your things right there by the door," Kate said.

She pointed to a box that was pushed up against the wall right next to me. It had my books, toiletries, some movies and CD's. There was a large black trash bag next to it filled with my clothes. *No wonder I hadn't felt like it was my apartment: all of my possessions fit into a plastic bag and one 19x17 inch box!*

"If I find anything else of yours I'll mail it to you," she said.

"Is it okay if I check the—

"Please just leave," she said, "I'll take care of it later."

Her voice sounded cold and dead. Her face was expressionless. It seemed as if all her spirit had been sucked out; like she was a shell of her former self—one that viewed the world through an entirely different lens, and no longer needed oxygen to breath. Any hint of care and consideration she usually addressed me with was completely gone.

"Bye," I said.

She didn't say a word back to me. Not even a look, gesture, or a noise.

I went to sleep at my parent's house that night with my tail between my legs and a shocked, depressed heart. My parents asked what had happened and I told them that Kate and I got into a little fight — no big deal.

I didn't tell them we'd broken up. For four weeks, I didn't tell anyone we'd broken up. I guess I didn't want to let it sink in and drag me into the hell Kate had seemed to go to so quickly. Plus, I imagined that we might reconcile, or drift back together again like we had the previous time. So if anyone ever asked me about her, I'd say she was 'fine' or 'pretty good' as I lingered in denial, and hoped the pain would never make it to my depths; hoped it would fade away somehow.

Since then I'd emailed her and texted, but she never responded. The night we broke up, four weeks before, was the last time I'd seen or talked to Kate.

When I made it over the last Mission Bay bridge, I got off the main road and hiked down the slope to the unpopulated path that hugged the bayside. When I felt out of public sight, on the sand and facing the water, I cried. It was a real cry. It was a pent up and delayed cry that should've happened the night we broke up.

Zonies

I guess it was around 5:30 or 6 when it started sprinkling. Rain wasn't in the forecast that day — or ever — but ominous clouds were overhead. I pulled my sweatshirt hood over my head and hoped the sprinkles wouldn't turn into full-blown showers. I stayed on the pedestrian route that hugged the water and winded along the sandy bay, straight into Pacific Beach.

I followed that bayside path to a small park that connected to the road again, and I looked back at the darkening bay. It was as if I were peering into it for some kind of present truth; some kind of immediate answer. Then, suddenly, I jerked forward because my left foot had run straight into cement. A big crack in the sidewalk, jutting up over two inches, almost sent me face first to the ground. Luckily, I was agile enough to recover without breaking my hip or having to use my hands to break the fall. There was only a brief moment of stumbling embarrassment. But my heart was beating three times faster while I checked to see if anyone had witnessed my klutziness.

When I scanned the area I noticed a family of five by the sidewalk ahead of me, hurriedly packing up their car with beach gear. They all had on bright yellow Arizona State Sun Devils T-shirts, as if they were sponsored by the school. They must have been at the beach for the sunset, then fled when they realized the sun was gone and felt a few raindrops.

As I passed them, I eyed their Arizona license plate. It reminded me that many San Diegans ridiculed and blamed "Zonies" for invading their space during the summer months. Some targeted the Zonies and made them the butt of their jokes. Some treated the Zonies as unwelcome immigrants, adding to traffic, congestion, and bad fashion sense.

I'm guessing those same San Diegans who scorned the Zonies considered themselves "natives." I doubt many of them considered the fact that there were only a handful of real natives left in the area (i.e. the Kumeyaay). I wondered if they — the San Diegans and the Zonies — ever considered that we were all immigrants here.

Kate was an immigrant too — from the East Coast. She came from New Jersey, like many San Diego transplants, seeking something new, sunny and fun in those vibrant years between college and real responsibility. Built-in to her California, party-filled, sun-worshipping dream was the traditional, unspoken intention of finding a husband somewhere between the beaches, bars and work. The next step would be the American dream — the whole shebang — a big house, nice car, 2.5 kids, and a healthy 401k.

Kate never mentioned anything about marriage plans for two and half years, but it was likely all part of a calculated effort to avoid freaking me out. So much for that effort, I thought. And despite the cold break-up and the lack of communication and all, I knew Kate was a great person — kind, loving, interesting and engaging. She was attractive enough and my family liked her.

So as I entered the heart of Pacific Beach, where Kate and I had made plans to meet, I had to ask my self 'Why?' *Why didn't I want to get married to her? Why did the thought of taking that path seem so regrettable?*

Maybe it was because the circumstances didn't make me feel particularly special. Had I just happened to come into her life at the right (or wrong) time? Sure, there was genuine love, but she was also ready to marry the next decent guy who walked through the door. And I was clueless at the time — clueless about her master plan as well as her effort to mask it all.

Maybe it was race and culture related? After all, Kate was a white girl from Jersey and I was a half-Mexican guy from a border town. I once found out that her mom called me "the Mexican boyfriend" when I wasn't around. I also remembered when her mom once asked if both my parents were Mexican and she whispered "Mexican" as if it were a bad word. Once, I felt awkward in a Mexican restaurant when Kate asked me certain questions about Mexican culture. She'd ask things like: 'How's a tortilla made?' Or 'How do you say this in Spanish?' Or 'How do Mexicans feel about…?' — How the hell was I supposed to know? I didn't even feel Mexican half the time — whatever being 'Mexican' really meant. And she knew I couldn't speak Spanish or make tortillas.

On top of that, there was my personal crusade against Kate's infatuation with the American dream. But as these thoughts trickled through my mind, my reasons for not wanting to marry Kate felt more and more like a weak, theoretical stretch. It sounded like a psycho-sociological academic book title: *Race, Culture, and the Rejection of the American Dream — by Frank Diego Rodriquez.* The reality was that even if I had written that book in a grand effort to explain our break up, and Kate actually took the time to read it, she'd only remember and focus on one word: Rejection.

Or maybe it was superficial on my part. I remembered Kate's self-tanning lotion that gave her a golden shimmer. It looked fake, smelled bad and tasted disgusting. I recalled her gooey lip-gloss that was so sticky it made kissing unappealing; her ridiculously expensive jeans that were especially designed to cover up flaws and tightly package that which was not tight. I admitted that after a year, any attraction to her body that once existed had completely faded.

Maybe I'd grown tired of her materialism — the value she placed on clothing and name brands, make-up, jewelry, furniture, housing, cars, fancy restaurants, and countless accessories. I wouldn't miss her love of those things either.

But were any of these solid reasons why we broke up? Weren't they all just different versions of things that would come up in any relationship?

A few raindrops hit my cheeks, turning into a steady shower as I tried to come up with one concise, simple answer to why Kate and I had broken up:

For me, it was a case of love that had faded; grown tired and predictable. And in the process, Kate had become much more of an intimate friend than a romantic girlfriend. It was the thought of being in such a dispassionate union with her — while teaching the same exact history classes over and over again for the rest of my life — that bored me to death. In fact, I had already started to feel half-dead long before the marriage question even came up, and that consistent feeling of passive indifference had scared me more than anything.

Of course, I couldn't say that to her, I thought. What would be the use? I imagined she'd only become more upset and disappointed with me.

The nauseous feeling I'd briefly had in the bus came over me again, returning in full force, along with a headache. The rain came down harder. The sky had turned three shades darker. I picked up the pace, not wanting to get drenched. I knew if I didn't move fast my sweatshirt would soon be sopping wet. I started to jog and my shins immediately felt the burn of a full day of walking. My feet and knees felt heavy each time my shoes hit the soaked cement. And the nausea wasn't going away either.

I cut down the alley. Then a feverish chill ran through me. No longer able to deny my sudden illness, I slowed and came to a stop under an empty carport. I coughed uncontrollably, which turned into gagging. That's when I began to vomit and lunged, pointing my face away from the carport, as if I was trying to make it into an imaginary toilet. I grasped my knee with one hand and the edge of a small loading dock with the other. As my stomach tensed, my rib cage heaved and my eyes watered with every contraction and expulsion. It felt like an exorcism.

And while I gasped for air in between intervals of throwing up my lunch, I noticed a lone piece of graffiti on the dirty gray wall right next to me. It said this:

Zonies Suck Balls!

Javabucks

I hovered there, drooling and spitting for a minute, trying to clear my mouth of its putrid remnants. But it was no use. I wiped my lips with my wet sleeve and kept walking down the alley, pretending I was fine. With a scraggly beard and a soggy dark sweatshirt on, I probably looked like a bona fide homeless man.

My vision was blurred and my body was sore after the puking — which must have been brought on by a full day in transit, barely any water, and some unexpected running. But it could have just as easily been brought on by the truth about me and Kate.

It continued to rain, but my attention was focused on the hydrochloric acid stuck to the roof of my mouth. I couldn't clear it out, no matter how many times I coughed and spit. I needed to rinse immediately, so I turned out of the alley and onto the main street that dissected PB: Garnet Avenue. The street eventually led to Gringos, which was the second to last building before the boardwalk, sand, and the Pacific Ocean. But that wasn't for another six or seven blocks.

I spotted a Javabucks on the left and made a beeline.

Light-headed and nearly drenched, I strolled into what seemed to be the driest, closest place I could wash my mouth out, sit down and recover for a minute or two. I was in Javabucks — of all places — where I found myself listening to the acoustic pop flavor of the month, and being scrutinized by the attentive manager. I could feel his stare before I even looked in his direction. His expression revealed disgust at my appearance and I assumed he was pegging me as a vagrant. True: I was far from presentable at that moment. I was disheveled, wet, un-groomed and heading straight for the bathroom. But the unisex bathroom door was locked. So I stood there and waited, checking my clothes to make sure there were no signs of puke.

I glanced around at the familiar, corporate Javabucks interior design and then up at the menu. *Coffee?* — That's the last thing I'd put in my stomach. *Water?* — A much better idea, but asking for a free cup would probably confirm my apparent bum status. Paying three bucks for a deluxe bottle of water might make me a damn fool, but I was ready to make that admission in order to buy time to pull myself together on a dry, comfy chair.

When the bathroom door opened, I rushed in without making eye contact with the stocky Javabucks employee who I guessed had been taking an extra five minute break on the can.

Before the door closed behind me, I stuck my head in the sink, splashing water on my tongue and my face. I swished tap water through my mouth and spit. I did this repeatedly. I took as much water as I could cup in my hands and rinsed a half a dozen more times.

When my mouth was almost back to normal, I paused and looked in the mirror. Water dripped from my face onto my beard. My eyes were bloodshot, and the bags underneath them were more prominent than usual. I spotted a few gray hairs by my left temple. Throughout the day I had reminisced and envisioned myself much younger than the person staring back at me in the mirror. I dried my face with rough paper towels and exited the bathroom, feeling a little cleaner yet older than before.

I sat down in a Javabucks club chair and could feel three pairs of employee eyes upon me. As a slew of unwelcome stares seemed to come from all angles of the room, I felt like the Unabomber and wished I were back in the private confines of the bathroom. *Don't worry,* I thought, *I'll buy something from you petty bastards. I'm just waiting for the rain to die down.* I knew I was a getting a bit defensive, but I was usually good at keeping those feelings well hidden.

I made myself comfortable and sunk into the fake leather cushions. I gazed out the window. I couldn't help but look outside in unwarranted anticipation of my parents, a friend, Kate — anyone — randomly driving by, noticing me, picking me up, and ending this godforsaken day the easy way. *Would Kate even pick me up, or acknowledge my existence?*

Everything would be fine, I hoped, but my stomach was beginning to feel weak and empty. I considered the possibility that I wasn't thinking straight anymore. I knew I needed to drink water or eat something because I felt like I could pass out right there in Javabucks.

"Excuse me, sir," said a slender man who approached me in a green apron, black polo shirt and Javabucks hat.

I guessed he called me sir out of habit, or because of Javabuck's policy, rather than out of sincere politeness. His next words indicated that he hadn't the least bit of compassion or respect for a guy like me.

"I'm gonna' have to ask you to leave now," he said.

Did he just tell me…? No, it must have been a simple misunderstanding.

"Oh, I was just about to buy something," I said with assurance.

"Nope, you're outta' here buddy. Get up," he said.

Really? He went from "sir" to condescending "buddy", then a direct command? And it hit me that he actually thought I was a bum. The insult was more shocking and ridiculous than painful. I almost reacted by correcting his misconception, but something about my state of mind, something about my unorthodox day made me embrace the role instead.

"I didn't know this place was so Fascist." I said.

It was too much, I admit. But my bold comment brought his attention from the bottom of my dirty pant leg back to my face. He looked at me with weary eyes, as if I might be some kind of lunatic.

"Please, just leave, buddy," he said to me.

I paused to read his face. I sensed my lack of immediate response producing a tense silence. I'd never been mistaken for a bum before and was kind of curious how this guy might continue to mistreat me.

"'Buddy'? You're certainly not treating me like a buddy," I said, with more politeness than I was feeling. Then to compensate I added, with an uncharacteristic tone, "Who owns this place anyway, Mussolini?"

In retrospect the Italian World War II references were excessive — probably unnecessary — but it had been a long day.

All Mr. Frappacino did in response was stare at me. He wasn't the only one. As I glanced around the room, it felt like every person inside Javabucks was staring at me now. I imagined being viewed as the crazy homeless man — the loony speaking jibberish to himself on the trolley. I couldn't believe it. *I should have left right after I'd washed out my mouth in the bathroom sink. Or should I? I was a goddamn human being, no matter what I looked like. What gave them the right to treat me like this?*

I wanted to give a speech about discrimination, or prejudice, or the history of the Civil Rights movement — anything to smack some sense into that roomful of coffee-sipping spectators and armchair judges. *Brown vs. Board! Rosa Parks! MLK!* But as I scanned their scornful eyes, especially Frappacino's, I figured it would all fall on deaf ears. I'd be dismissed as a crazy bum who looked white to some people and Mexican to others, spitting historical references about black people he knew nothing about. So I didn't say another word.

The silence was definitely awkward.

As I walked around the Javabucks manager on my way out, I almost muttered something about not wanting to spend three dollars on a bottle of water anyway, and how the idea of selling water was ludicrous, and how he was a superficial bastard. But I realized that might prompt the authorities to bring out the straightjacket.

So I exited quietly.

Gestapo

The rain had almost stopped. I decided to walk down the alley to avoid the imagined judgment of others on the way to my destination.

That's when I started gagging again. It hurt. My stomach cramped. Empty, it felt like it was eating itself. I hunched over and didn't move for a while. *Was this the symptom of something more serious? Was it a new viral epidemic that had yet to sweep the national news?* My insides grumbled and tightened in pain. I would have given up and called Kate from a pay phone at that point, but I had never memorized her number. Stored numbers in dead cell phones aren't very useful.

Still hunched over in my vomit-ready stance, I heard tiny gravel rocks grinding under the tires of a car not too far behind me. But I stayed bent over without turning my head to look. My insides were aching, my hands on my knees; my eyes on the unstable ground. The pain was enough to ignore the presence of anything that didn't seem to be a remedy. A car couldn't end my discomfort, so I paid no attention to it. I spit a bit more, but that was it — nothing else was coming out.

From the reflection on the dumpster, I saw that flashing red and blue lights were coming from the car that had just pulled up. *The police? Who were they looking for? They couldn't possibly have issue with me. I didn't do anything.*

I might not have looked like the most upstanding citizen at that moment, but I was no criminal. *Had I broken any law I was unaware of? Maybe Frappacino or some other employee at the coffee shop had called the cops on me, but that seemed unlikely.*

I heard the car door shut and the heavy footsteps of boots walking on soaked gravel. I slowly straightened my back and turned to face him.

"You okay there, partner?" said the officer, then more harshly, "Hey, amigo, let's see those hands."

Was he really talking to me? Of course he was, he was looking right at me. I was the only other person in sight. Partner? Amigo? Was this a bad spaghetti Western? Was I about to be arrested by a sorry excuse for John Wayne?

When the officer stopped about five feet in front of me, I could see the details of his pasty face. He looked young and anxious to prove himself. That's when I began to feel like a Mexican outlaw in a 1970's Western movie. You know, the one who'd be played by a white actor — with a pancho, sombrero, fake black beard and tequila flask in hand. I was that character casually leaning against the old saloon's wooden porch railing. And I'd probably take a bullet early in the shootout, but nobody would care. I was the bad guy technically — the Mexican guy being played by the white dude. The audience only really cared about Clint Eastwood or John Wayne, and cops like the young guy in front of me — who was looking antsy while he waited for me to answer his stupid question. Then his hand slid down to his pistol.

"I said, are you okay there?" he asked me.

"Yeah. I'm fine, thanks," I said.

"Hey, watch the attitude," the cop warned.

I didn't think I had said it with a saucy tone. I intended no disrespect.

"Sorry, I'm just feeling a little sick," I said.

"Yeah, sick of all that cheap whiskey, huh." he said.

"Excuse me?" I replied.

"Who said *you* could ask any questions here, bud," the cop said.

"I'm just feeling a bit sick to my stomach. No whiskey." I said.

"Shut your smart-ass mouth," he snapped, "You're only to speak when spoken to!"

"I'm sorry," I said, "I don't see anyone else around here, so I assumed you were talking to me." Then my disgruntled alter ego added: "And since when did the *Gestapo* take over here?"

It sounded like another man's voice coming out of my mouth. *Gestapo?* Had I really said that? It was like I had climbed out of my body and was watching this jackass named Frank challenge a police officer in a dark alley.

"Put your hands on your head and turn around right now!" he ordered, with his hand gripping his gun. "Am I gonna' have to cuff you?"

It was not a Western movie scene. And it was really happening to me—not a stunt double. I followed his directions, but at a much slower rate than I normally would. I was being treated as a criminal for some odd reason, so I began to act the part. Plus, I was acutely aware of my cramping stomach with every slight movement.

And it bugged me that this rookie cop earning his stripes in PB wasn't protecting or serving in the least.

"Have I broken some law I'm unaware of?" I asked, with my back to him.

"You don't ask the questions here, I do!" he barked.

"Really, what's up with the Gestapo tactics?" I asked, with my hands still above my head.

I felt a bit more justified saying it the second time. *Since when were you unable to speak to police officers or ask basic questions?*

"What did you say?" he asked as if I had said the unthinkable; a forbidden word. He inched closer.

I realized at that moment he could have been angry with me for a number of reasons: 1) I had asked another question which was against his rules, 2) He was deeply offended by my associating him with the infamous Nazi secret police, or 3) *Gestapo* was a historical reference outside his range of knowledge and he simply didn't understand what I had just said.

Then I said something *really* stupid, which might have infuriated him for two of the reasons listed above—and confirmed that I was nearing some kind of delirium.

I asked: "Do you even know what the Gestap—

Before I could finish my question, the cop grabbed my hands and violently handcuffed my wrists behind my back. But the cuffs weren't even metal. They were heavy-duty plastic ties that made me feel like a newly tagged animal.

"Son of a bitch," he said, as he pushed me toward the flashing lights, then crammed my non-resistant body into the back of his squad car. It all happened very fast. He'd made me a criminal in a matter of seconds, and dared to insult my mother in the process.

This rookie cop was a real cockbag, and I wanted to call him just that but I knew it would only make the situation worse. He obviously had no ability to listen anyway. And for whatever reason, normal powers of speech had abandoned me once he'd cuffed me. Perhaps it was the musty smell of the backseat of that police car, or the shock that I had been arrested. No, it wasn't a movie or a game, I thought, because if it were, then I had clearly lost. *The end. El fin.*

Soon the police car was moving, which wasn't good for my stomach or the upholstery. My insides were still in bad condition. Scratchy radio noises and code numbers were coming from the speaker built into the dashboard. It sounded like two guys playing with walkie-talkies, pretending they were cops. After a few minutes of keeping my mouth shut, I took a deep breath and decided to put an end to my predicament with a new approach.

"Can I ask you a question, officer? I said.

"What's the point?" he said.

"Am I being arrested for calling you 'Gestapo'?"

"Gah-what?" He asked.

Jesus Christ, he arrested me just for asking questions! He didn't even know what 'Gestapo' meant. Did the police academy train people how to not think?

"I mean," I said, "Did someone from Javabucks call you?"

"I can't disclose that information to you," he said, as if the words 'disclose' and 'information' made him superior—legally above any sniveling question from a commoner, a homeless peon like myself. I waited a minute, adjusting my approach yet again.

"May I ask why you've arrested me, sir?" I asked.

"May I?" he mocked. "What are you, an English teacher or something?"

"Close," I said. "I teach history. I'm a profess—"

"Oh, yeah, sure," he interrupted, "a drunk and disorderly teach—professor, huh?" I might as well have told him I was the mayor of San Diego.

"An adjunct professor at Belmont College. Yes," I said, feeling a bit more embarrassment than pride.

"What's your name?" the police officer asked with a hint of interest. Maybe he had begun to notice that I was neither inebriated nor incoherent.

"Frank." I said.

"Full name, please."

"Francisco Diego Rodriguez."

I didn't roll the R's like I should've because I couldn't.

But what did any of it matter, I thought. It appeared that my master plan for the day was a lost cause. I was under arrest and on my way to jail. The mechanic's shop would be closing soon; the tentative meeting with Kate dropped.

"That's a mouthful," the cop said.

He didn't attempt to repeat my name, but I was used to that. However, I wasn't used to being put in jail for no reason. This wasn't how my day was supposed to end. True, my plan had failed. It had become a comedy of errors, but I was too close to the finish line to accept total defeat. Hearing that I was a professor seemed to spark the cop's interest for a moment, but it had quickly disappeared.

Our silence was renewed for a few minutes, only to be disrupted by the CB radio's beeps, scratches, and indecipherable cop-speak. I closed my eyes in frustration as the squad car cruised south, out of PB.

Was there anything that could get this robotic dickhead to change course? His 'drunk and disorderly professor' comment reverberated in my ear, but it was inaccurate. He'd rushed to judgment, and it had all happened too fast. He was an amateur. He hadn't even —

"Yes, I'm an American history professor," I said out of the blue, hoping he would listen. "In fact, we were just discussing the significance of the 1966 Miranda Supreme Court decision in class the other day. You know, the reason why the police have to read citizens their rights before they arrest them."

The cop didn't say a word for a few seconds. *Would it work?* Officer Wayne, despite his lack of critical thinking skills, must have realized that he had skipped a few steps in his overexcited attempt to throw me in the drunk tank. In fact, he was legally in the wrong. He turned down the volume of the cross-talking radio.

"And?" he cued.

Rather than faking a Tom Cruise attorney bit while reminding him of his constitutional duty to read people their rights, I explained my unusual daylong journey, my vomiting episode, the scene in Javabucks, and my plans to get my car and meet my so-called girlfriend. I gave him the short version. He listened as he drove. Surprisingly, he never cut me off.

Before I had finished my explanation, he made an abrupt U-turn. But he said nothing about it. Up until that point, I'm sure he had his mind set on driving me to jail and tossing me in with the other drunks — or wherever they put homeless guys who talked back to cops. Over the course of ten minutes, he had changed his mind.

When we made it back to almost the same spot the cop had unofficially arrested me, he pulled over. He parked halfway on the sidewalk as though parking laws didn't apply to him. He didn't say a word when he opened the back door, led me out more carefully than he'd thrown me in, and un-plastic-cuffed me. I stood there on the sidewalk, expecting him to say something, but he waited until he'd made it back to his driver's side door, shook his head, and said:

"Adios, amigo."

It echoed in my head long after he'd driven away. *Could he fathom that somebody with a Spanish-sounding name couldn't even speak Spanish? "Amigo?" Did I look Mexican to him, or did he say that to everyone?* It seemed like a joke: Me, standing on the side of the road looking destitute and desperate, with faint plastic cuff imprints on my wrists, wondering how the hell I made it to that point — motionless; surreal.

That's when I peered down the street and saw the restaurant's name cut out in stylish, rusted, brown metal, illuminating one word: *Gringos.*

Gringos

I decided to go into Gringos first to ask what time it was. Maybe I could still pick up my car, I thought. If it was too late for that, I could at least wait for Kate, unless she was already there.

The second I stepped inside Gringos, I was greeted by a beautiful blonde hostess. She looked at me somewhat suspiciously as I approached her podium, and I had a quick flashback. I didn't want this to be Javabucks all over again. So I removed my hooded sweatshirt in order to feature my dry polo short underneath. Polo shirts commanded respect, I thought — especially the ones with the real logo on them. I glanced down at the little yellow polo player on my chest for reassurance.

The hostess's cute smirk didn't ring of feigned kindness. In truth, it seemed more like an attempt to hold back laughter at my shabby, disheveled appearance.

"Nice shirt," she said.

"Thanks," I said. It worked — or so I liked to think. Her eyes sparkled along with the faint amount of glitter in her makeup.

"Will you be dining with us tonight?" she asked.

"I'm meeting someone here." I said.

"Do you wanna' wait at the bar?"

"Sure," I said.

She pointed me in the right direction.

I was always amazed at the décor in restaurant-bars like Gringos. The amount of money spent on pricey knick-knacks and exotic accessories—even the employees' uniforms—were designed to perfectly fit the American image of what rustic, "authentic" Mexican should be. To be honest, it seemed just non-Mexican enough—not colorful or loud or well used enough—to make the typical Southern California patron feel comfortable and trustworthy of the setting, inflated prices, and watered down cuisine.

It was a bit too polished and posh, which made me feel uncomfortable. But that couldn't distract me. If it did—with one inappropriate comment or harsh historical reference—I might end up in the back of another police car.

I perched myself on a stool at the bar and scanned the room for Kate. She wasn't there. Within seconds, a well-groomed, clean-shaven bartender skipped over to my spot and placed a Corona coaster next to my hand. He greeted me with a big smile.

"Hola, Amigo!" he said.

His hard pronunciation of the 'H' in 'Hola' revealed that his Spanish was even worse than mine.

I hesitated, then replied: "Como estas?"

"Oh, you speak Spanish?" he said.

Apparently 'hola' and 'amigo' were the extent of his fluency.

"No," I said, wishing it weren't the truth. "How about you? How's your Spanish?"

"Horrible," he said. "But they tell us to throw in some Spanish words here and there, when we can — you know — it's a very Mexican place."

"Yes, *very*. I can see that," I said.

"So, what are you drinkin', amigo?"

"Water," I said.

The Nile

When a grown man sitting alone at a bar asks for a water as his first drink, the bartender may rightfully display an expression of bewilderment, or at least a fair sense of disappointment. This guy kept it on the positive.

"Going clean tonight, huh?" he asked.

"Yeah, sort of," I said.

"Don't wanna' pull a Stephen Johnson tonight?" he asked.

Stephen Johnson was a professional football player in San Diego. Aside from getting paid millions to catch a rapidly thrown object amidst enormous men paid to knock his head off, Johnson was known for going out to local clubs, drinking excessive amounts of alcohol, then drunk-driving and getting caught.

Go Chargers!

"Something like that," I said. But I didn't know why I responded so flippantly. My situation was nothing like Stephen Johnson's. "I'm here to meet my girlfriend," I added. It was still easier to just say "girlfriend." No need for explanations that way. It had become a habit, I suppose. I asked the bartender: "You know what time it is?"

"Oh, about 7:15," he said, as he leaned away from me, circulating to attend to other customers.

Goddammit! I couldn't believe it. My temporary arrest had made me miss my date with Kate and it was now too late to pick up my car. Jesus Christ! The whole point of the day had been blown, I thought. I sunk my face into my hands. My entire day had become an unequivocal failure.

"What time were you supposed to meet her?" the bartender asked.

He'd unexpectedly turned his attention back to me and put my water on the coaster. He seemed like a friendly guy — polite and inquisitive — but I wasn't ready for his questions. I didn't want to talk. I felt like a deflated balloon lying on the bar, pathetic on many levels.

"At 7," I said.

"Maybe she's late," he suggested.

"She's never late. I'm always the late one."

"Why don't you call her?" he asked.

"I don't know her number," I said.

"What?" he said in disbelief.

"My cell phone's dead," I explained.

"Oh."

His surprise was erased. He understood that people didn't memorize numbers anymore. Yet I found it odd that his interest in my situation was above that of an average bartender.

"What's she look like?" he asked.

"Average size, brunette, cute, I guess... Her name's Kate."

"I guess"?

The bartender must have read my mind.

"Hey, man, make sure you don't ever describe your girlfriend like that to her face," he said.

My eyes fell to the perspiring glass of ice water in front of me. I didn't respond. I couldn't. Funny that a thing as simple as breathing can become so difficult all of a sudden. I drifted into a momentary abyss with the bartender's last prepositional phrase: *to her face*. Again, it reminded me that I hadn't seen Kate face to face in four weeks.

"I haven't actually seen her for weeks," I divulged to the bartender in a half shamed voice.

"What?" he asked. "Are you sure she's still your girlfriend, man?"

No, we broke up! Do I have to spell it out, amigo?

The breathing part was slowly coming back, though the heaviness remained. I paused for a moment and then pulled my focus back to the bartender's doubtful, concerned eyes.

"I'm not sure," I said. But in that moment I *was* sure — certain that my relationship with Kate was finished — done. Which also explained the physical pain I'd been experiencing.

The bartender sighed.

"No offense, bro. I'm no psychologist," he said, "But it sounds like you're either joking, on medication right now, or in denial — big time."

Then he drifted down the bar to another Gringos patron.

I winced. My stomach cramped again. I was reminded of my recent stomach condition. It had improved, but still hurt. The realization of denial hurt much more.

Denial.

It reminded me of a kid named Juan and my first teaching job. Juan was a 6th grade student who once told me a corny pun. It happened when I was teaching his class about ancient Egypt. I was referring to the Nile River a lot that day, so when the class was over Juan told me:

"Mr. Rodgriguez."

He pronounced my name with a perfect accent.

"De-Nile is not just a river in Egypt," he said.

And I wondered if he'd just heard that line in a cartoon, or if he was a prophet trying to tell me something I would only realize ten years later as I sat on a barstool in a place called Gringos.

Kate once told me about a real trip she took up the Nile River in Egypt. She said she ate something bad on board, and became violently ill for the remainder of the three day voyage. I remember her describing the pain as a hell that sounded ten times worse than my recent vomiting scenario. But when did she go on that trip? Why Egypt? Who was she with? How long was she sick for?

I didn't know any details because I had never really asked her enough questions.

I'd spent most of our relationship asking *myself* questions like: Why didn't I feel that she was the one?

When had she stopped being physically attractive to me? And, could she ever be in Playboy magazine, even on a good day? And so on.

That was the problem:

I was the problem.

That's why we had broken up over four weeks ago. And I'd been paddling up the Nile ever since.

Days Off

I guess you could say it all came crumbling down on that barstool in Gringos. The bartender had somehow opened me up, and I wasn't even drinking — nor was he probing too deeply. I was just sick and tired — exhausted from lying to myself, I suppose.

It had worked for four weeks, but I couldn't do it anymore. I couldn't continue this way, and my failed day of walking through the city had somehow helped put my face to the fire. I was finally confronting the truth — about Kate, my profession, and my life: all of it.

I pictured the silver tequila bottle behind the bar talking to me with a cartoonish Mexican accent: *'Escucha: No more personal history or distracting commentary, professor. Can you even call yourself a professor anymore? Remember the history department meeting, Frank?'*

At the end of my last faculty meeting at Belmont College, Margot — the department chair — said: "Consider it more days off."

She had said the exact same thing a year before when each adjunct professor's number of classes was reduced because of state budget cuts. I remember a few professors chuckled at Margot's sad attempt at humor. Most didn't find it funny in the slightest. We all had bills to pay, and some had families to support. But we grudgingly accepted the news. What else could we do? It was no secret that the economy had worsened. The recession had arrived and all financial news was bad news. The state and federal governments were deeply in debt, and education budgets had to be cut drastically. Everyone knew this.

At the beginning of last semester, one of the elder adjunct professors joked in our first meeting:

"Margot, are you gonna' tell us we have more *days off* again?"

Nobody laughed.

"There's just no money," Margot said helplessly, "And, yes. Unfortunately, for most of us, there will be more days off."

At the end of last semester, just before Kate and I broke up, there was no department meeting for me to attend. I simply received an email from the department chair that explained, in detail, the horrible financial situation of the state and federal governments. It was filled with depressing statistics and attempts at consolation, explaining how ancillary academic programs and benefits had been cut in order to preserve at least *some* teaching jobs.

It was hard to swallow. Maybe because it never mentioned the students' welfare — nor the teachers'. Maybe because it didn't mention that the government allotted billions more to military expenditures than to education.

The email ended, as it should have, with a bitter quip:

"So it looks like more days off!"

Well, the new semester had already started, and I hadn't worked a day in six weeks. But I'd still been calling them "days off" to my friends, family, and even myself — mostly because it was easier than explaining my unemployment. But also because of my delusional hope that they'd be calling me soon, in need of a teacher or a substitute.

The bartender returned to me and asked: "Are you ready for a real drink, man?"

"Tequila shot, please," I said.

It was a knee-jerk response. The words left my mouth without thinking at all. And it may have sounded like one of the dumber decisions I'd made during a day filled with questionable choices, but it ended up working in my favor.

"Wow, what's the occasion — things looking up?" the bartender said.

"Getting worse, actually, but thanks for asking," I said.

He poured me the shot and made one for himself too.

"Cheers to my day off," I said with a straight face.

"And to your *girlfriend* too?" he asked.

I had to laugh. I couldn't help it. It was either that or start to cry.

After downing the tequila, sucking on a lime, and praying it would help attack any acids left lingering in my stomach, I thanked the bartender and stood up. I handed him my last wad of one-dollar bills but he wouldn't accept them. He stuck out his hand and we shook and exchanged glances. Then I thanked him a couple times before heading to the door.

Never Text

I smiled flirtatiously at the hostess as I passed through the entry way. She shot me a quick wink that seemed more second-nature than especially designed for me. I would have winked back, but I never learned how to do that. They say it comes naturally to some people.

Not me.

So I just squinted my left eye as I passed her, then turned to the front door with my head pointed down. When I went to push the right side open I pushed at thin air because someone else was pulling it from the outside. I looked up from the handle.

It was Kate.

My heart froze.

Time froze.

I froze.

I couldn't bring myself to speak because my throat felt like a damp towel being rung out all of a sudden — way worse than the breathing difficulty I'd had beforehand at the bar.

She looked at me like I was the village idiot. Her wide-open eyes made the lines in her forehead more prominent. I was speechless. *Where was I supposed to start?*

"Are you gonna say anything?" She spoke with little sense of patience. "You *are* the one who invited me here."

"I thought maybe you'd already left," I said, in a barely recognizable voice. "I didn't even know if you'd come."

"Wow, you have quite a beard there," Kate said, changing the subject. And with a hint of disgust, she scanned the rest of me for any other visible flaws.

"I knew you would be late," she added. Of course she had to use this crucial moment to point out one of my bad habits. "That's the only reason why *I'm* late," she continued. "So where are *you* going?"

"I realized —"

" — Oh, another realization, huh," she said as she rolled her eyes, unaware that interrupting me had become one of her bad habits, and one of my pet peeves in our relationship.

She opened her purse with a great sense of urgency, and pulled out a piece of lined paper that had been folded into a little square. She held it out in front of me as exhibit A.

"Do you remember this?" she asked.

"I don't think so," I said.

"Of course you don't," she replied.

She was noticeably upset. It was as if *I* had broken up with her and boxed her possessions at the door — not the other way around. She unfolded the paper, almost frantically. Kate read the note out loud:

Dear Kate,

You have made me realize so much about myself. I have taken your love for granted, and I will never do so again. I realize now how important and special our relationship is and forever will be. I love you.

Love, Frank

"You wrote that!" she reminded me.

"I know," I said, embarrassed at the lack of depth and poor style. I remembered that the note had accompanied some flowers I'd given her after she made me feel guilty for hanging out with my friends a lot during one weekend when I needed a break from her. Kate's control sensor and insecurity light must have been triggered sometime that weekend. I must have thrown in "forever" as a gesture, not as a promise to marry her. And part of me probably knew, way back then, that I wasn't compatible with her expectations; that our dreams were incongruous. I was more confused back then, and ignorant of my placating ways; my denial.

How could I explain this to her now though? What would be the point? Wouldn't it just piss her off more?

Then I stared into her eyes and lost myself for a moment, like I usually did. *Would I always be consumed by what she might be thinking and feeling, and then act in compliance with that?* It was part of my old problem: *Tell her what she wants to hear. Make her happy.* Maybe that's why we had been together for so long. Maybe that's why I'd never complained. Because if we ever really did begin to open up, then our whole relationship began to look more like a complicated friendship to me.

"I realized," I said, "I think I've been in denial."

"You think?" she said sarcastically. She liked to be sarcastic.

"Well, I'm a little slow," I admitted.

"Tell me about it. You've texted me almost every day since we broke up."

She sighed in exasperation. She reminded me that "text" was now a verb — which still bothered me. Her intensity made me think of how she'd made me feel when we were together — like I was on a clock and had to say something sophisticated, yet conciliatory and comforting all in few seconds, or she'd walk away.

"Well?" she said.

I felt the pressure. It reminded me of the pressure Kate routinely applied. The way she ordered for me at restaurants before I could finish saying, 'I'll have the….' The way she planned out our entire day before I even woke up. The way she assumed we would spend every waking moment of non-work time together. The way she embedded the idea of marriage and kids and a home without ever saying it directly. It was her dream — or the dream that had been inculcated in her since birth.

Maybe all the pressure she put on herself to acquire that dream had manifested into pressuring *me*. And even though it was over between us, the tension still mounted with the simple fact of her presence.

"You know, I didn't really come here to have dinner with you," she said.

"No?" I feigned surprise but knew I hadn't planned on eating dinner with her either. Frankly, I couldn't afford it.

"No. I came here to tell you to *never* text me again," she said, "For closure."

She *would* use the word "never" — so absolute. She *would* use the word "closure." It sounded like part of some lame line from a Jennifer Anniston movie she'd forced me to watch. It definitely wasn't her word. I didn't think she wasn't creative enough to explain any of this in her own words.

But I didn't have the balls or the ability to explain myself either. My sense of time and space was too surreal, as if I were stoned. One minute passed too slowly, but the next whizzed by.

I thought about it: *Closure.* Though it hurt — that is, the end of denial and the acceptance of finality — it all made much more sense while she stood there in front of me.

I looked at the post that held up the Gringos sign. The base was made out of fake stone that was cracking. The pole was rusty. I fixated on it for only a moment, but it seemed much longer.

"Okay," I finally said, in response to the 'never text' request.

"'Okay' — that's it?" Kate said.

"Yeah." I said. *Was that it?*

"Are you sure?" she pressured.

She clearly wanted more, but I couldn't give her any more. She needed closure — that was all. She didn't want me to explain my personal reflections on how I'd been distracting myself from my own problems; from our failing relationship; from my lack of true happiness. She didn't want to hear about our differences and my reinterpretation of the American Dream.

She'd interrupt me anyways. She'd roll her eyes. She would try to control my speech, and I might fold and revert to the compliant appeaser who didn't want to hurt anyone, even if it meant denial, outright lying and — eventually — hurting someone. That much was clear. And it was still pretty hard for me to speak.

"Yeah, that's it," I said. "You're right. We shouldn't be together."

That's all I could get out of my mouth. And I barely got that last, clipped sentence in there without having my voice crack. But after uttering those few words, I felt the weight of three years sliding free. I adjusted my sweatshirt in my arm and took a deep breath. I was ready to walk away from her.

But neither of us walked away.

Kate just stood there and shook her head at me in disappointment — maybe even disgust. She looked cold, calculating, disconnected — hell-bent on getting her way and controlling the situation. At the very least, controlling herself. She revealed no outward signs of emotion — no compassion — only a desire to win the argument (if there was one); to persuade me of my fault in the matter and assume her righteousness.

It reminded me of the night we broke up. I had selectively forgotten the event until that afternoon. I had done so in favor of romantic nostalgia, old pictures together; my highlight reel. Memory had smoothed the jagged edges.

Now it was over, both in my heart and my mind. It had been over for more than four weeks, but I finally knew why.

"No more texts." She repeated.

No, I thought. I would never text her again. She didn't need to worry about that.

I nodded and said: "Be good."

I'm still not sure why I said that, of all things. Then again, it must have subconsciously meant that—since our relationship was clearly over—I hoped she wouldn't run out and have passionate wild sex with the first guy the cat dragged in. And maybe my comment was appropriate because this was her response:

"Be safe."

She said it like a command, but I'm guessing it meant the same exact thing as 'Be good.'

And then Kate spoke the last words that I ever heard come out of her mouth and that I, coincidentally, completely disagreed with.

She said: "You know, you never can be too safe."

And these were my last words to her:

"Yes, you can."

Death and Life

I felt better — more like myself — as I walked away from Kate. She reminded me why — when the subject of marriage came up — I had doubted and delayed, and couldn't bring myself to lie about something so big. And I think it crushed her. But it had gotten to the point where I was, in fact, wasting her time. And nobody wants to have their time wasted, nor to be considered a waste of time.

Closure had definitely happened. But I hated the word "closure", so I called it "death" instead. It sounded more morbid and tragic — as most deaths are — but, like a diseased elderly person who requests a family member to pull the plug after years on a life support system, also a relief. Thus, the sadness of finality was accompanied by a fresh breath, which was probably why I didn't sob uncontrollably or break down as I walked along Mission Boulevard.

I was heading straight to the mechanic's shop where my car was. I assumed the place would be closed, but I had to check. I had to try. I hoped for the unlikelihood that there would be an employee or two still there, willing to make an exception for me. More importantly, it seemed that with every step I took toward that mechanic's, a part of my old self was shedding.

I suppose it had been happening all day, but it was becoming more obvious to me. It was as though I was disrobing layers that Kate had imposed on me, unhealthy habits I had accumulated, negative attitudes I had cultivated, and the subtle misery of indifference I had concealed for so long. I imagined it all falling off of me and onto the wet sidewalk.

And some very basic questions began to float to the forefront: *What's the next step? What do I want to do with the rest of my life? What's limiting me? Why am I here?* These were existential questions, and I had to admit that I had no answers. I felt like the stupidest unemployed professor in town.

Though I lacked solid answers, and by most American standards I would be considered a consummate failure, I realized those questions were now swirling inside me because of one reassuring fact: *I was free.* Nothing was stopping me anymore. There were no plans or obligations—no duties or pressing responsibilities. I had no girlfriend or wife—no dependents. I had no job, and the job market was far from promising. So I had nothing to lose.

And what had the day taught me? —Carl, who marched with Martin Luther King, had been around the country and the world. Natalie, with her energy and audacity, was pursuing her true artistic interests. Che was speaking his truth. The Runner was globetrotting. Even Miss Saigon was trilingual and had made it across the Pacific Ocean from Vietnam. Yet I was born and raised in San Diego and had never lived outside of Southern California, which suddenly seemed like a tiny fraction of the world.

Ushered in with the day's events was a new-found appreciation of one simple fact: *I was alive.* I was also healthy, and felt I had gained a new type of sanity (one that might have been labeled "crazy" by others). I kind of felt like one of those recovered alcoholics, or druggies, who become invigorated by the simple fact that they're still alive after all that drug abuse; after all of that self-inflicted pain.

Endless possibilities were opening up. And for whatever reason, the spirit of the moment had me fixated on physically moving to another place — another country even. *Italy? Japan? Mexico? — but how?* Sure, I could've started over with a new mindset right here in San Diego, but it wouldn't be a truly clean slate. It wouldn't necessitate redefinition and complete independence.

I recognized that I had to leave town to be truly reborn; to truly grow. I learned, in that brief walk to the mechanic's, that part of me had died, and I needed to make a drastic move before I could genuinely begin a new phase of life.

Enrique's Deal

There I stood, finally, in front of the shop: *PB Auto Repair*. They specialized in Volkswagens. Their neon sign was off and their gate was locked, but I saw one light on inside the garage. I could see my car parked twenty feet away, in the middle of two rows of cars, behind a tall, locked, chain link fence. Normally, I would've shrugged my shoulders and tried again the next morning. But I wasn't going to give up that easily.

I picked up some loose, muddy gravel next to the sidewalk and threw a pebble at the only garage window that was illuminated. No response. *Who was I annoying in there? Was there anyone inside? Little pebbles wouldn't damage the window, right?* Then I threw a few more. The rattling noise they made was a bit louder, but still no response. I picked up some more pebbles and—while I was cocking my arm to throw—the door next to the garage swung open violently. A wide-bodied, dark-skinned Mexican guy stormed out with a large wrench in his hand.

"What the hell's your problem, man?" he yelled.

I would have normally been frightened by his bulldog appearance, but there was a metallic barrier between us and three padlocks keeping it shut. With the time it would take to open them all, I'd be able to run away. And I was sure I could out run this guy. Really, I was just hoping he'd calm down a bit so I could plead my case.

"Sorry," I said, "It's that I spent all day trying to get here to get my car and—"

" — We're closed, bro!" he said, shaking his head.

He was clearly agitated. Maybe the pebble throwing was salt in the wound of a long day of hard manual labor. I noticed that despite his Mexican features, he didn't have a trace of a Mexican accent — pure Americano inflection.

"Is there any way — " I started.

" — No," he cut me off.

"You wouldn't believe wha — "

" — Nope." He said, and began to inch away from the gate.

"Okay, here's the thing —," I tried to restart.

"Hey man, here's *my* thing: I work on cars," he said. "I don't do the paper work, and the guy who usually does is gone. So I can't do anything for you, and I wouldn't anyways."

"Well," I said, "Can you at least tell him that Frank Rodriguez came by to get his Passat, but —

"Frank?" he squinted his eyes as he stepped toward me with a strangely renewed interest. He examined my face under the lamppost light. "Frank Diego?" He asked. "You went to Immaculate Conception, right?"

"Yeah," I said, curious and a bit freaked out about how this guy knew me. Nobody had called me "Frank Diego" since junior high. But I was also hopeful that whatever it was he recognized in me could get him to soften up and hand over my car.

"Yeah, I went there," I repeated.

"Oh shit, man, you used to play hoops with my brother in 8th grade," he said. "Back in the day."

His tone switched from irritated to interested — even excited.

"Jimmy Reyes — remember him?" he asked. "I'm his little brother, Enrique. I was three years behind you guys."

He said this with the enthusiasm of a child who still cherished the opportunity to be included in any activity with his older brother and his friends.

"Oh yeah, I remember Jimmy," I lied.

I had no idea who this mechanic's brother — Jimmy — was. Maybe he was a bench warmer, or in another class, or just a quiet, unmemorable kid. My last year at Immaculate Conception seemed like a distant snapshot of incomplete memories, but I needed to milk this Jimmy connection. Enrique, a few years my junior, looked completely unfamiliar too. But he was the key to my car, and my car was the only mobility — the only valuable possession — I had in the world.

Though what would I do with my car if I was going to move to another country?

"Yeah man, you tore up that championship basketball game," Enrique gushed, "I remember you made a half-court shot *and* scored the game-winning basket. Man, that was tight. I'll never forget that."

"Wow, good memory," I said.

I could barely remember that game. It was so long ago — back when I had unknowingly reached the apex of my athletic glory. 8th grade was the last year I excelled in any sport.

"Hey man, sorry about coming out here all pissed off." Enrique said. "I didn't know it was you, Frank, and I had a long day, ya' know."

I sighed an understanding sigh and smiled. "Yeah, no problem. I know. It's been a long day." I said.

"Yours is that Black Passat, right?" Enrique spotted it in the row of parked cars. "You know, I really like that model and year. Really cool and classy... Let me go grab the keys to open this gate."

As Ricky walked back to the office, I wondered if I even wanted my car anymore. *If I was gonna' leave the country, wouldn't it make more sense to sell it and take the money? I would need the money. And I'd paid off the loan just months before. But how long would it take to sell the car? Two, three weeks? I didn't want to wait. I'd already deferred this for too long.*

Ricky returned and went to work on opening the padlocks. "Let's see if we can get this Passat back to you tonight," he said.

"I thought the guy who does that was gone?" I said. "Now you're acting like you own the place."

I didn't like the way it came out. I must have reverted back for a moment, sounding like my cocky junior high self. But Enrique didn't seem to mind.

"Yeah, sorry about that. I kinda' lied to you earlier. Come on in." he said.

It immediately made me feel better about lying about remembering his brother. We ambled toward my car.

"Actually, I *do* own this place." He said.

"Oh, you do?" I said with some surprise.

"Well, yeah, I co-own it with two other friends," Enrique explained. "We all went in on it together, and now it's sort of a cooperative where we all share equally, even the newer employees."

"Wow, that's great," I said, impressed.

"I worked on your car personally, man," he said, pointing to it. "It's in great shape. I love that model." He looked it over, checking out the bumper and hood. "It's a few years old, but the engine's great. It has low miles too," he said. "Passats were made well that year, huh."

I nodded in agreement. I was sure he had specific, perfectly good, mechanical reasons why it was a well-made car; why it was a good year; why the engine was great. I didn't. I didn't have a clue about cars. "You wanna' buy it?" I asked him.

Enrique turned toward me with a look of shock and perhaps some intrigue.

"Are you serious, man," he asked and then stopped himself automatically, "No, I can't."

"Yes, you can, Enrique" I said, as if I'd known him for years and sold used cars everyday. "I'll give you a very good price because I'm about to leave San Diego and I want to get rid of it."

"I can't," he repeated, but his tone was unconvincing. I could tell he was thinking about it.

"That car's worth about $12,000 on the market," he said, "I don't have that kind of spare money in my wallet."

"I'll sell it to you right now for $8,000," I offered. "Preferably in cash."

I didn't have to explain the upsides of the deal. He was already many steps ahead of me in the process. He knew the car and its resale value much better than me. He knew he could turn around and make at least a $3,000 profit. He also knew, as a co-owner of a business, that he could go into the safe deposit box inside the shop and get the cash, no problem — assuming they had a safe deposit box with lots of cash.

"You have the title and registration?" he asked.

"In the glove box." I said.

He walked away from me to look more closely at my car. I was glad it was nighttime. Most of the scratches and nicks were invisible. My car looked pretty good, even though it was five years old.

"Kinda' looks like a Beamer," Enrique commented.

After some surprisingly brief deliberation, Enrique decided to buy it for $9,000 to be fair to his former 8th grade hero. "I'll take it, Frank. It's a steal," he said, as he motioned me into his garage.

We both sat down in his messy, oil-smelling office. Enrique whipped up a generic contract and I signed the title and a few other forms, all while he reminisced about some other athletic exploits of mine that I had either forgotten or remembered much differently. After ten minutes — like that — the deal was done. He put the cash in an envelope and handed it to me. We shook hands.

"Thank you, Enrique," I said gratefully, not yet absorbing what I'd done. He had no idea how timely this sale was.

"No problem, man," he said, "Thank *you*. You just gave me the deal of the century… And it's Ricky," he added, "People call me Ricky now."

I gave him a gracious smile, turned, and walked out the door. Ricky followed me out to lock the gate.

"Is everything okay, man?" he asked.

"What do you mean?" I said.

"I mean you just sold your car for hella' cheap in like twenty minutes. Is there some kinda' rush?"

"Well, I want to leave the country as soon as possible," I said.

"Man, did you commit some crazy crime or something?" He asked, chuckling to himself.

"No," I said, "It's just time for me to move."

"Oh yeah. Where you going?"

"I'm thinking Mexico," I said. It felt good coming out of my mouth so spontaneously and for the first time.

"Pues, que tengas un buen viaje," Ricky said.

That was the only time he indicated he could speak any Spanish whatsoever. But he sounded fluent after saying that phrase. I was pretty sure it meant "Have a good trip."

Ricky added: "Hey, I bet they'll call you 'Francisco' down there, man."

He was probably right—*Francisco*. I liked the way it sounded with the right accent. And I always envied the ability of some San Diegans to jump in and out of Spanish and English when it best suited them. Maybe I'd have enough time in Mexico to learn how to do that too.

I thanked Ricky again, told him to say hello to his brother (whose face and name remained a total mystery to me), and speed walked away with one hand firmly holding the envelope inside my bulging pocket full of ninety one hundred dollar bills.

Operation Mexico

Because of my day-long, crash course in public transportation, I knew exactly where I was going and how to get there: back on the #9 bus to the Old Town trolley station and then onto the red line south to the Mexican border. The bus stop was only a few blocks away, so I wasn't worried about getting there. I was only worried about getting down to Mexico without any major glitches.

I imagined it as "Operation Mexico." The idea had flashed though my mind a few times that day: once on the trolley for a moment, after sitting next to the Runner, then on the short walk to the mechanic's. I had thought about it many times before that, but never with the conviction or will to actually do it.

A large part of the appeal of Operation Mexico was the spontaneity of the mission. *Just keep going South – don't stop. Don't look back.* I checked the hidden pocket inside my backpack where I hoped I'd left my passport. It was there.

Operation Mexico wasn't like Operation Playboy. That was something that kept me content, distracted, and tied to the same place. Instead, the move to Mexico would give me true independence, starting a new life in a different country with $9,000 to get me going. I knew it wasn't a fortune, but in Mexico that could go a long way.

Maybe it was my Yaqui instinct, but I decided I had to start the operation immediately. I didn't want to go home to grab any clothes or toiletries. That might stifle my momentum. I knew that if I stopped at home I might have changed my mind. I might have seen a picture or a friend or been reminded of an obligation of some sort that would temper my impulses. And I supposed there wasn't anything I needed that I couldn't buy in Mexico. *It wasn't a different planet or a deserted island. They had grocery stores and pharmacies and clothes there that would fit me just fine.*

The mission was simple: to safely transport myself and my small fortune deep into Mexico and find a nice, warm, coastal town with a healthy supply of tacos and beer. I could learn some Spanish. I'd have time to read and write what I wanted to. From there I would figure out the rest. I guessed my wad of money could last about six months, maybe more.

A Dangerous Man

The bus ride back to the trolley station felt shorter, the way the drive back always feels shorter for some reason. It was good that it was brief because it didn't give me much time to second-guess my decision to leave the country without any further delay.

The ride to Old Town made the last part of my day seem like a flash: a brief episode that was being rewound—the vomiting in the alley, the walk along the bay, the Sea World stop where I ditched the bus. The images drifted by, all under the darkness of night and the lightly trafficked streets. The bus was empty and quiet. No Miss Saigons or young aspiring poets to talk to or observe.

When I arrived at the Old Town transit center, I remembered what happened to Raul there only a few hours earlier. I looked around for government agents as if it was illegal for me—an ex-professor with no criminal record and no commitments—to escape into Mexico with $9,000; as if some intelligence agency or secret police force was tracking me and on to my plan.

I checked the dimly lit schedule to see that the red line would depart in a few minutes. I walked toward the idle trolley cars and kept my hand in my pocket, always on my money. I realized I'd never carried that much cash before. I wondered if some of the guys lurking in the shadows or waiting on benches were eyeing the bulging cash in my pocket. Preoccupied with it, I noticed the top of the envelope was visible, creeping out of my jeans, so I pushed it deeper into my pocket.

" —Still don't know where you going, huh?" said a deep voice from about twenty feet away.

At the sound of that voice my heart jumped and remained suspended somewhere near the top of my throat. It more than startled me. My life savings was in my pocket. I decided that if I had to defend myself and fight to protect my money, I would. It was my ticket to a new life abroad. I turned to my left, where the voice came from, and saw an older black man sitting down peacefully on a bench. It looked like Carl. *What were the chances?*

"Is that you, Carl?" I asked.

"Yes, sir," he said. "You look kinda' jumpy for a full grown man with a full grown beard walking around here after dark."

"Just being a little extra cautious, that's all," I said.

"A little caution is good," Carl said. "But too much can end your life before it even starts."

He stood up and came closer to me. He continued talking before I had a chance to respond.

"Know where you going yet?" He asked.

"Mexico," I said.

"Oh, that's a beautiful country — hot!" Carl said. "I used to live down there for about two years with a little senorita — down on the beach. Mmmmm."

I smiled at him in disbelief. It seemed that Carl had done just about everything everywhere and I would never know the half of it.

"Wow, you didn't say anything about Mexico this morning," Carl continued, "You have an epiphany today, or what?"

"Yeah, I guess you could say that." I said.

I wanted to say more. I wanted to explain to Carl my entire day and what I learned about myself, as if he was a trusted counselor or psychologist — not a man I'd met briefly on the trolley that morning. I wanted advice from Carl, who seemed to have lived a vibrant, experience-rich life. I wanted him to pull out a pamphlet with all the answers to life's biggest questions.

"Well, an epiphany can truly be great..." he said.

I smiled with pride.

"...Or it could be a big load a' cuss," Carl finished.

My expression flattened.

"Only time will tell brotha'. Time will tell," he repeated confidently.

Silence filled the space for a few moments, with Carl likely thinking about old times, grinning knowingly to himself, while I only hoped that experience and the passage of time would make me grin the same way some day.

"And where're you going, Carl?" I asked, as if it was something more than a perfunctory question.

"Home," he said. "My wife is probably worried sick. I haven't talked to her since my cell phone died this morning."

I guessed there were two kinds of modern communication types out there: the people who let their cell phones die, and those who didn't. My phone was already dead and about to be put to rest for quite some time. And I felt pretty good about it. *Call me a Luddite.*

"You got a plan?" He returned the attention to me.

"My only plan right now is to get to the border, cross smoothly, and get south of TJ without any problems," I said.

"Problems? What kinda' problems you anticipating?" he asked.

I realized that I hadn't told him about the money in my pocket. There was no reason to. It would've either sparked more interest and financial advice than I wanted, or struck him as a laughably small amount to flee with, and I didn't want the embarrassment.

"You know, bad guys, criminals, TJ… the border's a very dangerous place." I said.

"Not as dangerous as you," Carl told me.

I squinted at him, confused.

"Look at yourself, man. You're a grown adult who looks on the brink of homelessness — on the edge. The only reason I don't think you're homeless now is cause I talked to you this mornin'."

He laughed at himself, paused and refocused — not on my shabby clothes and thick beard, but on my eyes.

"You're the dangerous one," Carl told me and then clarified in a louder voice, "But I don't mean in no Van

Damm, Rambo, Jason Bourne bad-ass way or nothing like that."

I admit, I kind of thought he meant the bad-ass way for a second. I'd seen too many movies and had looked up to those kinds of dumb, muscle bound heroes my entire childhood.

"In what way then?" I asked.

"I mean," he said, "The most dangerous threat to you, is *you*."

Carl paused to let it sink in a bit.

"You control your destiny, son — you. Never let fear control you and what you do," he said. "If I'd let fear control me I'd still be wasting away in Alabama — or found dead face down in a river, or some jungle in Vietnam. But no. No sir, I'm livin'. Livin' in sunny Southern California, being alive, being me everyday. It doesn't matter how old you are either."

I listened intently, thankful that Carl was Carl, and that I had the chance to talk to him twice that day; wishing we could chat and I could absorb some more, but also knowing that I had to leave.

"Remember that: The danger lies in you, man," he went on. "Other people gonna' see that beard and them raggedy clothes, and they're not gonna' give a cuss about you. Just like most people — not really caring too much about anyone but themselves. So do your thing, whatever it is, whatever it needs to be. Be true to it and you'll be fine."

"Thank you, Carl." I said.

"Oh, yeah, and remember: Don't drink the tap water," he said. "Don't even brush your teeth with it, man."

"I know." I said.

And it occurred to me that I already knew a lot of the pieces of advice and lessons that Carl and others had given me that day. It was just that I hadn't been seeing, articulating, or living them out.

The lead car of the approaching red trolley pointed north, but would soon be curving east, toward my parent's house. It came to a stop. Carl turned to it.

"The blue line. That's my trolley," he said, "Now you better get on yours. It leaves here in about a minute."

He pointed toward my trolley on the other side of the tracks. We shook hands, but I needed to ask him one last question—as cheesy as it may have sounded:

"Carl, why have you been so... nice to me today?"

"Oh, you mean besides being old?" he said.

"Yeah," I said.

"You're searching for something, man. But you don't know what it is." Carl paused, smiled and said: "I like that."

And I could have turned around and left feeling good about myself with that as Carl's last comment, but he wasn't quite done. His final few words showed he wanted me to chew on something a bit different.

"But do me a favor though," Carl added. "Don't use the searching thing as an excuse. If you *searching*, yeah, you'll always be looking for answers, but don't let it be an escape from reality. Let it be a way to become a better person."

I wasn't expecting that from Carl. But the words *excuse* and *escape* have resonated in my ears ever since then. I thanked him for speaking the truth, and wanted to tell him how much I appreciated his wisdom, but there was no time for that. We just nodded, waved at each other, and parted ways.

He went east toward home.

I went south toward an epiphany.

Dominic V. Carrillo is a teacher and freelance writer from San Diego, California. He began creative writing as a graduate student at UCLA. He currently divides his teaching and writing time between California, Italy, and Nigeria. For contact information and more about his current projects visit:
www.tobefrankdiego.com

CPSIA information can be obtained at www.ICGtesting.com
Printed in the USA
LVOW10s1440150813

348092LV00016B/454/P